Groundwood Books is grateful for the opportunity to share stories and make books on the Traditional Territory of many Nations, including the Anishinabeg, the Wendat and the Haudenosaunee. It is also the Treaty Lands of the Mississaugas of the Credit. In partnership with Indigenous writers, illustrators, editors and translators, we commit to publishing stories that reflect the experiences of Indigenous Peoples. For more about our work and values, visit us at groundwoodbooks.com.

GO HOME

GO HOME

TERRY FARISH AND LOCHAN SHARMA

Groundwood Books
House of Anansi Press
Toronto / Berkeley

Published in 2024 by Groundwood Books / House of Anansi Press
groundwoodbooks.com

We gratefully acknowledge for their financial support of our publishing program the Canada Council for the Arts, the Ontario Arts Council and the Government of Canada.

 Canada Council for the Arts **Conseil des Arts du Canada**  **ONTARIO ARTS COUNCIL** **CONSEIL DES ARTS DE L'ONTARIO** an Ontario government agency un organisme du gouvernement de l'Ontario

With the participation of the Government of Canada
Avec la participation du gouvernement du Canada | **Canadä**

Credits: 28 from "Rock Me, Mama" (1973), later called "Wagon Wheel" (2004) by Bob Dylan and Ketch Secor; 65 from "Saathi" by Yama Buddha, 2011, distributed by Songs of Nepal, English lyrics Genius.com; 76 from *The Book of Questions* by Pablo Neruda, translated by William O'Daly, bilingual edition, Copper Canyon, 2001; 157 from "Make My Day" by Coi Leray and David Guetta, from *Coi*, 2023; 186 and 221 from "Soldiers" by Adrian Patrick, *True Love Never Dies*, 2012.

Library and Archives Canada Cataloguing in Publication

Title: Go home / Terry Farish and Lochan Sharma.
Names: Farish, Terry, author. | Sharma, Lochan, author.
Identifiers: Canadiana (print) 20230575897 | Canadiana (ebook) 20230575919 |
ISBN 9781773069104 (hardcover) | ISBN 9781773069111 (EPUB)
Subjects: LCGFT: Novels.
Classification: LCC PZ7.F22713 Go 2024 | DDC j813/.54—dc23

Jacket illustration by Shonagh Rae
Design by Michael Solomon
Printed and bound in Canada

Groundwood Books is a Global Certified Accessible™ (GCA by Benetech) publisher. An ebook version of this book that meets stringent accessibility standards is available to students and readers with print disabilities.

Groundwood Books is committed to protecting our natural environment. This book is made of material from well-managed FSC®-certified forests, recycled materials and other controlled sources.

MIX
Paper | Supporting responsible forestry
FSC www.fsc.org **FSC® C016245**

1

OLIVE

Olive pedaled from her house in Creek Village, past the Day Night Store at the traffic light, and west into the country to Gabe Boudreau's house. He lived in the sticks.

They all lived on fingers of land built up with ashes and stones and probably whatever washed in from the sea. Olive's brother, Chris, always said they were just borrowing this land from the sea that surrounded them on the New Hampshire Seacoast.

"Hey, Olive," Simone called. Gabe's kid sister was a businesslike eight-year-old. She hung Olive's helmet by its chin strap over her handlebar. She pulled Olive past the chickens and out to the dirt-bike track Gabe had built with a sandbagged perimeter.

Simone smelled like grass and mud and little-girl sweat.

"It's almost summer. You got a job yet?" Olive said. She wore her hair in a messy fat braid and now bunched it up to get it off her sweaty neck.

"Silly," Simone whispered. "But I do have a secret."

"What?"

"You'll see. Also, I'm learning jumps." Simone clamped on her boots with ankle guards, shin guards, calf guards.

"You amaze me," Olive said.

"I know," Simone said. "Why don't you move here? You and Gabe are like puffins."

"What do you know about puffins?"

"They mate for life." Simone tucked her chin down and lifted her gaze to Olive. Gabe and Olive had known each other all their lives and had been together a solid year.

Gaudy little chickens jerked their feathery selves around them.

Olive didn't like chickens. Sometimes she pictured herself in a city job with fine-tipped pastel markers and open-toed heels. She and Gabe knew they were going to have different kinds of jobs. They liked that. And then they'd get to come home to each other.

When they were kids, she and Gabe and her brother covered the city on their bikes, from Creek Village, where the working-class families lived on the north side of the river. Or they rumbled across the lift bridge to the south side and a whole other world of the tourists and the swanky who lived in the big houses they could barricade from the sea when it rose.

Now here came Gabe in a spiral of sun. Simone wrapped her small fingers through Olive's.

"You can watch me jump. Gabe built jumps with piles of dirt."

"Coming," Olive said, but her eyes were on Gabe. She liked watching his eyes take in a problem and crush it. She knew the smartest people were dirt-bike racers like Gabe. Enduro racing made them into engineers.

Now he stood there in shredded cutoffs looking like sand and sky with his thick, beach-brown hair and his blue eyes.

"Where you been?" he said. He was eighteen, older than Olive, who had one week left of her junior year.

"You're making fun 'cause I'm a schoolkid." A smile she couldn't hold in spread across her face.

Simone took her bike off the stand. Her hair flew in the wind behind her and she headed to the track.

Gabe was beside Olive, his mouth over her eyes and her cheeks and her mouth. She felt his hand under the fine silver chain she wore at her throat, like even that couldn't separate them.

She'd keep a herd of chickens for this boy.

Nero, a cross between a Great Dane and a flop-eared hound, loped out to Olive, yelping with dog joy.

"New ones are Barred Rocks," Gabe said, pointing to some chicks.

Olive's fingers found the loops of his jeans. "You ever stop working?"

"Not so's you'd notice," he said.

That was the Boudreaus.

They set to work together. Laid a new bed of hay for the cluckers, filled a low trough with water the chicks could reach. Hosed down the vegetable garden. Wrestled with the hose until they were both completely wet and their hair fell over their faces. They sprawled in the hay like puppies showing their bellies.

Behind the nearby pines, Simone was kicking up dust around the track.

"How many days left of school?" he whispered.

"Four."

"Move out here."

Her body said yes.

They stayed in the grass and warm sun, and their bodies fit together like the sea and the sky.

Finally, they sprang up and headed to the Boudreaus' front porch, which was overgrown with tangles of vines. In the kitchen, Gabe and Olive started supper to help out his mom who worked at Home Depot. This was how it would be when they had their own place and their own kids.

Olive glazed the crust of a frozen chicken pot pie with beaten egg to make it yellow-golden and shiny. Gabe watched her. They both knew this was a Chris technique, and it was like a sign that Olive being with Gabe was all right.

With the pie in the oven, Olive settled her cheek beside his jaw and touched the freckles on his straight lips. He wrapped his arm around her waist.

"Someday I'll build you a whole house," he said. "A brand-new house."

"We'll be okay wherever."

"There's a manager's job opening at the bike shop."

"You don't have to take another job." Olive took plates and forks to the table.

"It's a decent job. If I get it, I'll leave the gas station. Stick with me." He held her with an oven mitt on his hand. "God, I love your eyes. Dirt brown. You're the fuckin' earth to me."

She shoved him. "Dirt! You're the farm boy."

When the pie was good and crispy golden, they sat around a knot-holed table by the sliding screen door. They could smell the pine forest and see the orange flash of an oriole. Julia, his mom, had come home and dropped her long body in a chair. Her face scrunched up in a yawn.

"Fecking unending day."

"Here, then." Gabe, sitting across from her, got up and mounded chicken pie on her plate.

She lifted her eyes to him. They were tired and crinkled and searing blue like his. But her whole face took him in, and she said, "I always liked you."

"Hey, you, too, Mom." Gabe gave her a small salute, and a dimple showed.

Simone scraped open the screen door, and when she pulled off her helmet, her blonde hair dropped down. They all broke into the pie. Olive sat between Gabe and his mom, and she and Gabe wrapped their feet around each other's under the table.

"Remember the last time I made a real pot pie?" Julia asked. "Damn if the bottom of that old casserole dish didn't give way and that pie dropped right to the floor."

"I remember," Simone said. "We were watching me on TV at the protest."

Gabe sprawled with his arms reaching over the backs of the chairs on both sides of him.

"Simone carried a sign as big as her," he said. "Hold the line with me, kid." That easy smile.

Olive remembered the news footage. She'd watched it with her brother. Simone had been at an anti-immigrant rally with Gabe and Kyle, their dad, carrying a sign: *This is our country. Think of your children.* Olive could read most of Kyle's T-shirt. *Keep New England ...* The last word was hidden, but she knew it was *White*.

"What do they mean, think of your children?" Olive had asked her brother.

"It means spook 'em," he'd said from under his cap. "Scare people, you got 'em."

Just for a second at the table, Simone had worry in her eyes looking at Olive. Olive knew Simone was Gabe's small hit man. If anybody crossed Gabe, Simone saw it. Sometimes she'd had that worry when Chris and Gabe talked.

"He's my brother." A milk mustache dotted across the little indent above her lip like Gabe's. "You're supposed to be true to your family. If you don't have your family, who are you?"

Gabe leaned in toward Olive and brushed crumbly piecrust off a loop of her braid. He leaned back with that same straight smile, like he just liked the sight of her. She let him look, and her eyes laughed.

"You guys." Simone rolled out of her chair.

Everybody laughed. Then talk slowed down. Nero fell asleep out flat at Gabe's chair. An owl called from the woods. The chickens stopped their racket, tucked their tail feathers in for the night.

Julia's chin started to drop to her broad chest.

"Wait. Don't go to sleep!" Simone said. "I have a surprise. Come on!" She opened the sliding screen door.

It was going on eight but the days were long, and an eerie light was in the sky.

Julia sighed. "Oh, baby, I'm tired." But Simone looked like an angel in that light. They all trudged out into the stillness.

Julia touched Olive's hand.

"You look like the moon," Julia said. "All white and curved over my son with your head there on his shoulder."

Olive realized her shorts were white. Her shirt was white with small white straps that barely stayed on her shoulders.

"Here we are," Simone sang. "I made it."

In the center of the dirt-bike track was a wire creation, and from the wire hung seashells and beads and other mysteries.

"It's a wind chime," Simone said. "For Chris."

Olive felt her heart stop.

The shells clicked in the wind. Other things Olive couldn't see clearly. Were those little pendants made out of jar caps? Simone had glued on old photos of Olive's brother.

Around them all, a dozen battery-powered tower candles lit pictures of her brother in his canvas jacket that Olive now wore to school.

"I wanted to make you happy," Simone said. "'Cause it's June and it's the one-year anniversary."

Olive still froze.

"It's nice." Gabe broke the spell.

Olive stepped forward.

"Thank you," she whispered. She could have picked up the candles and smashed them into the field rocks like grenades. She avoided throwing up.

Olive put her palms across Simone's hands. Simone

thought this up all herself, the little girl who had buried her dead pets in solemn ceremonies.

Olive felt Gabe's large hands over hers. Julia wrapped her arms around them all. They made this knot in the middle of the dirt-bike track under the moon.

All of a sudden it was last summer. Last June. At Olive's house, back in the garage that Gabe and Chris had turned into a dirt-bike shop. Working on bikes was like religion. All the crap you could put on a bike.

But Chris was also an addict. And last June in the shop, he overdosed, and they couldn't bring him back.

After Julia and Simone went to bed, Olive and Gabe walked back out in the moonlight, past dirt-filled bags around the track. Then into the woods where Olive, Gabe and Chris used to go to call the owls.

Olive wanted to talk about Chris. Gabe didn't want to, but she did anyway.

"He talks to me," she said. "He just shows up and there he is, hanging out. Telling me what to do."

"Talks to me, too." Gabe's voice was hoarse.

"What's he say?"

"Usual bullshit."

"No, what's he say?"

"He says, 'Get the fuck outta here. Take a year.'"

She shoved back Gabe's cap so she could see his eyes in the moonlight. He had all the pain and anger from last June, right there, right back again.

He cupped his hands, let his thumbs lightly touch

to make a path for his breath. And then he whistled the barred owl's call. He got the rhythm and the pitch like Olive remembered. Four short syllables. *Who cooks for you?* Like Chris used to call.

Gabe pushed the white strap up on her shoulder and pressed his hands into her cheekbones.

"I'd come with you if you go," she said. She breathed with the feel of his mouth on hers.

"First, you want to bring some of your things out here?"

She nodded. "I'll tell Mom that's what we need to do."

An owl answered back. They stood still and quiet. The owl called again. And a third time.

Once was good. Olive didn't know about three.

2

SAMIR

Samir walked with his grandfather up the steps to the First Church of Christ thrift shop.

Hajurba stopped on the steps to watch a bike go by.

"We need to get a bike."

Samir said, "We're here for clothes."

They spoke in Nepali. Hajurba didn't know English. He liked to go to English class, but that was because his teacher had art materials. He drew his house in Bhutan, the rolling hills and the farm he had lost.

His grandfather didn't have art materials at the refugee camp. But some of the men shared a bicycle.

"Auntie Geeta gave us a list. You need a light jacket," Samir said.

"I will tell you a story," Hajurba said.

Samir was busy counting the money in his pocket. He dug in his shirt pocket and found Auntie's list. It was in Nepali. Samir had to fake it, reading the list. He didn't like to admit that he had started to forget how to read Nepali.

What was he supposed to get? He thought it was jacket, socks, something else.

They walked down a basement hallway and into a Sunday school classroom with suits and dresses on hangers and bins of neatly folded T-shirts and summer gear. He saw swimming suits, floats, Crocs.

Not far from his house, he had seen kids jump off the bridge into the creek ten feet down. He was terrified by the idea. He would die.

In the camp, he had learned break dance, Tamang Selo, Bollywood moves, hip-hop. His dance was like flying. But bodies of water made him sick with fear.

"We had five bikes in our hut in the camp." Hajurba was telling the story. Samir heard him, but he was looking for useful items among the neatly folded clothes for men. "Every night we bring the bicycles inside to keep safe from the locals. I was important," Hajurba said. "I had a vendor bike. I sold yogurt from the market. Very good yogurt."

"Hajurba, look at the jackets," Samir said. He waved his palm over a small rack of jackets behind the summer shirts. June nights could be cool for an old man.

"I hope for a bike," Hajurba said.

"Your old jacket is falling apart."

"In Bhutan I did not have a jacket. I have survived all my life without a jacket."

"In Worcester you needed a jacket."

But Hajurba returned to his story. "In the camp, whoever got up earliest got the best bike. Some bikes were not good. I always got up earliest so I could sell the yogurt."

Many people in the Sunday school room weaved through rows of tables spread with bright-colored shirts.

Samir and his sister, Heera, knew that when they came to New Hampshire, they would be with a lot of white people. Today he did not look into the white people's eyes and think of answers to their questions about where he came from.

Just get the jacket and get out. Baba needed Samir for a business meeting.

Samir held up a purple hoodie.

No.

"Or this?" Samir showed him a fleece jacket.

Hajurba did not look at it. He reached for a tan jacket with chest pockets and leather epaulets. His grandfather pushed his arms into the sleeves. He stood in front of Samir, his arms hanging loose by his sides, and a smile crossed into his eyes.

Samir had seen someone wear a jacket like this in a movie about a pilot. It could be a flying jacket.

"This one." Hajurba eased his shoulders back.

Samir led the way to the checkout. But Hajurba stopped at a table. He pushed things away with his large working-man's hands until he came to a pair of swimming trunks. On them were bright green parakeets with red beaks and ugly spiked leaves around them.

They knew this bird in Nepal, and Hajurba imitated their sound. *Screech-screech.*

Samir held back a laugh, but when he saw people looking, he dropped his gaze.

"Let's go," he said.

Hajurba picked up the parakeet trunks.

"For you," he said. "Here you will learn to swim and you will teach Heera so no one will drown in the river."

Samir put up his hands to ward off the trunks. "I'm all set."

But at the same time, he remembered the story of his grandmother. She was young in Hajurba's story. Samir had not paid much attention. She was one more ancestor who had died, and they had a special prayer for her as his father's mother.

Now Samir lived in a house in Creek Village beside so much water. Creeks, coves, a river as wide as a sea, bays. He had seen the Atlantic Ocean from a distance, even the sandy beach where he knew kids in his class would meet up on the last day of school and build firepits. He tried to not remember he was living now with so much water. And that made him feel a connection to what had happened to Hajurama.

Hajurba would not put the trunks down. Samir needed to go.

They took the jacket and the trunks to the checkout. Hajurba wouldn't take the jacket off, but he opened the trunks wide on the counter.

"Three dollars, total," the man said. "These have been around for a while."

Samir paid. He didn't pick up the trunks. Hajurba carefully rolled the trunks and slid them into one of the pockets of his new jacket. He smiled, and his yellow teeth showed his happiness.

They wound their way down the hallway and found a

room of outdoor things — plastic garden chairs, basketballs, a hoop to mount, tennis rackets.

Right in front of them — right in the middle of the Sunday school room — was a bicycle.

It was a middle-sized bike. Smaller than the bike of the girl who lived across the street from Samir. It was old. It didn't have gears. It had flakes of a gaudy yellow paint. This bike was once bright like a parakeet.

Hajurba approached it. "Even if I got up before anyone in the hut went to bed, I would never get a bike as good as this."

Hajurba was a slight man — five feet three inches. He mounted the bike and solemnly pedaled it down the hall.

It fit him okay and he didn't need to adjust the seat.

Auntie didn't say to get a bike. So many reasons to take it, though. Hajurba missed many people, and a bike could bring him joy. Baba, Uncle and Auntie were here, but Samir's ama and sister were still in Worcester while Ama finished up her restaurant certificate. Hajurba was only partly here without Ama and Heera. Sometimes his eyes glazed over, and Samir knew he wasn't here at all. He was with Hajurama in Bhutan.

"How much?" he asked the clerk.

"Twenty."

By now Hajurba on the bike was in the street.

"All right," Samir said.

Outside, Hajurba said, "I will take you to the river where my teacher took us. It might be a good place to learn to swim. A school is across the water."

"Where is this place?"

"Not far." Hajurba began to pedal.

Samir ran beside him. His felt the wind in his hair and the pumping in his legs. It felt good.

Hajurba in trousers and the flying jacket sailed through the streets of Mersea. They passed a fountain in the square. The fountain sprayed swirls of water the shape of an umbrella.

Samir texted Baba. "Hajurba wants to show me a place. Coming soon."

The square was a public place in Mersea where people could say what they wanted. They were allowed to have flags and bullhorns.

Baba had said, "It means this country has freedom. No one can do this in Bhutan."

Today a band of girls raised signs overhead and screamed, "If You Breathe Air, You Should Care." Drivers honked from their cars.

Samir followed Hajurba out of the city center, then another turn and another. Samir realized they were in a cemetery with new grass almost the color of the coriander Baba grew.

"How much farther?"

Finally, at the end of the cemetery, Hajurba pedaled into the woods on a path he somehow knew. They passed a forest pond. At the end of the trail was a new body of water Samir had not known to avoid. The river bulged out against a circle of land.

A cove.

They were alone. The land was scrubby. Water lapped the boulders and rocks on the shore. The wind blew the water in, and Samir could see the dark high-water mark on the roots of the trees.

"Okay, now let's go home," he said.

"Look." Hajurba pointed to a seagull over the water. Between the spur of land they stood on and a large bridge toward the east, there was a small island. On the island, Samir could see a rambling, broken-down building with long windows and a porch along the front.

"My teacher said this is a school," Hajurba said.

"It's a ruined building."

"Yes, now," Hajurba said. "But once nuns lived there and it was a good school. I think this is the school where the Kingdom of Bhutan sent the young prince."

"Hajurba, you have so many stories."

"Yes, maybe," he said. "But the prince did come to school in America. Why not here? He came in 1992. This was not a ruin then. It was graceful and beautiful and run by strict nuns so that all the students became engineers."

Samir shook his head. He was so late.

"You see, there is also a horse."

Yes, Samir could see a mostly white horse who looked like he was leaning against a wooden fence.

"He is good luck," Hajurba announced. "Horses always know the way home."

"You are a good storyteller, Hajurba," Samir said.

Baba had texted. "Where are you? This man doesn't know what I am saying."

Samir had to get Hajurba on the bike. "Do you know the way home?"

But Hajurba was not finished with his story. He turned to the broken-down school and the napping horse.

"I say if the king of Bhutan sent the prince to go to school in America, he must know what he is doing. So, I have sent my grandson to school in America." He gazed with his hand over his eyes in the glare of the sun at the former school on the island with a horse.

"I say my grandson is also a prince of Bhutan."

3

OLIVE

On Sunday, Olive rode through the cemetery on her way to meet Gabe at the cove. It was a place they'd gone with Chris. She slowed down through the windy rows between headstones.

It was late afternoon, and the sky threatened rain, and there came her brother out of the gray air. She nearly ran into a gravestone.

Chris!

She got off her bike, rested it against a sumac tree and watched. Let him come.

Chris was slow and deliberate, in a haze of weed.

He looked just like their dad — cow-eyed, slow-moving. He was so real. She could see his funny, gloomy eyes taking her in like she had never stopped amusing him.

He could make a boat skip over the waves. He was reading up on falcons when he died.

Real slow, they fell into step.

Hey, Chris?

Yup.

I'm tired of school. It drags on and on. I have a whole other year. You're not even around.

She didn't mention Gabe. How he was done with school, and she felt so done.

Well, it's up to you, he said, slow. *But then you'd never know what color your prom dress was.*

What? My prom dress?

They cracked up, because Olive dressed in striped shirts and Chris's old jackets, even if sometimes she glammed up with her friend Lise.

Five years ago, Chris was playing the ring-toss game at the county fair. He had a good eye and he won over and over. As a prize, he picked a set of stainless-steel spoons wrapped in a cloth, with a little pouch for each spoon.

Won this for you, Olive, he'd said.

What do I want with spoons? I'm eleven.

He just shrugged. *I'm setting you up for life.* His cow eyes glinted.

She thought maybe for Christmas he'd get her an iron.

She had kept the spoons in the same cloth bag.

I mean, I have the spoons, she reminded him now.

But he stopped.

Race you! she screamed to keep him longer.

But he disappeared. She reached her arms up to the dark clouds.

I'll quit school if I want! Her hair fell down her almost-bare back.

'Then she stuffed it in a baseball cap as rain fell down, and she ran.

Gabe had left his dirt bike in the parking lot at the head of the path. Olive saw his purple cap ahead in the mist. It said *Irving*, the gas station where he worked. It slid down when he wrapped her in his arms. His hands pressed her ribs under Chris's canvas jacket that smelled like a tent.

The bumper sticker on his bike — *America Is Full Go Home* — was old and peeling on the back fender like always. She pressed down the edges of the sticker out of habit.

They walked into the woods. Tangles of vines dropped from the trees, and rain streaked their faces. She didn't tell him Chris had come partway.

She hummed, "Rock me mama like a wagon wheel" — a song she'd learned from this old guy on YouTube. He had an episode called "Guitar Playing for Loneliness." He had said, *You know, it happens to all of us sometimes.* And then they dug in to where the fingers press the strings.

The rain was come and go.

Gabe's neck smelled like motor oil and bark. She kissed his couple-day-old scruffy bristles. "Rock me baby like the wind and the rain." Changing the words up.

They slowed a bit and walked with their arms tight around each other.

They came to the shore of the cove. Moving east, the river spilled into the Atlantic Ocean. But here in the middle of the cove was the small island Olive knew. Across the way on the shore of the island was a white spotted horse. Olive swept off her cap at the sight of him.

She used to see him as part of the landscape. She knew people on the mainland past the island could cross to it by a wooden bridge. It was people over there who rented the land for the horse to graze. They'd built him a lean-to.

"You're here, Lord of the Fishes!" she called.

Gabe's eyes softened. "You're banjo-eyed over an old horse."

"Remember how Chris and I called him Lord of the Fishes? There was something about the way he held his head, like he was lord of all this water and fish."

She whistled to him using two fingers — a way for Olive that involved a lot of spitting. But the wind carried the whistle and the horse lifted his head.

"It's me," she called. The horse stared at Olive, or at least he seemed to, for a good while. He shook his mane and whinnied back and the sound came.

Gabe looked too bone-tired to call to horses. When he could, he got on a pickup crew going out ground fishing. And he worked with his dad nailing roof shingles.

He held Olive's hand and pulled his cap low over his eyes.

"I've been thinking about Jackman," he said. "It's way up there, almost to Canada. We could paddle on the river. Get one of those fishing shacks and have picnics. Just to get away."

Get the fuck outta here, Chris had said.

Something about that white horse was keeping Chris as real as this rain. She could see him lift his hands like a preacher.

29

Then she smelled the oil on his hands and on the concrete of the garage floor.

Olive walked into the garage. First she brought water in a blue cup for Chris to drink. He looked pale and she sucked in a deep breath like if she did that, he'd do it, too. Chris, she said, you okay? Like she could coax him into it. She saw again the light shimmer of the blue glass.

But Gabe said to go get that spray she and Mom kept in the bathroom. Narcan. She must have raced into the house, but she didn't remember.

Second she brought the Narcan, ripping it out of the pack.

Gabe was talking all the time. Steady, steady. Walk with me. Chris was so groggy.

Did you call 911? His voice shook. She had the Narcan. Why had they taken so long? But they hadn't. It was a heartbeat.

She didn't remember calling, but Gabe said she had while he was telling her get the cap off.

Then Chris was on the ground. Olive was on her knees. She remembered how cool the concrete was. She had the cap off the nozzle. Gabe pushed it into one nostril, pressed the plunger. The left. Gabe was pressing his chest in a way Olive didn't know how to do. Chris wasn't breathing.

"If you don't have your family," Gabe said now, "what do you have?"

Stay with me, brother, Gabe said to Chris over and over in the garage.

Three minutes was a lifetime. Gabe plunged the spray into Chris's other nostril. The right. Now Chris would breathe himself back to the garage where he lay with bike grease on his neck.

But he didn't wake up. On the oil-stained concrete, his scruffy hair pressed into her hands.

On the beach, Olive shivered.

"It's too cold to swim," she said.

They kicked off their shoes in the dirt under an apple tree with sprawling limbs at the place where the beach met the woods. They sat on a tree trunk that had fallen across the tree's roots.

"He never had a chance," Gabe said.

Olive kept shivering.

"Come closer," he said.

She climbed up on him and felt his coarse jeans under her bare legs. She let go into him.

"Closer," he whispered.

They settled tight into the curve of the fallen tree.

That's when they saw the boy. He appeared in the haze. He must have been walking around the curve of the shore and just came into view. He was totally focused on the tide coming in, and he sprang from it like it was a snake.

Olive knew the boy because he was that new kid in her English class in January and, what's more, had moved in across the street. One day a fisherman lived there, and the next, a woman in a red sari and more people, including this kid, Samir. Gabe called him the alien. He didn't belong in the neighborhood. She knew him from Mr. Wyeth's class, but he was just the foreign kid.

Gabe's fingers closed down on her hand. She was wearing the ring Chris gave her with a turquoise stone, and his grip made the band dig into her skin.

"Wait here," he said.

"What do you mean, wait?"

Gabe ran out to the surf where the seawater was bubbling onto the rocky beach. Fat raindrops fell as the tide pulled in, and the sea took over the sand.

Samir must not have heard them. He wore flip-flops and tapped his right heel on the sand and stones at the edge. He was a little bowlegged. He stood with his feet wide, his hands crammed in his pockets. He wore his cap backwards.

Olive balanced between two rocks and wiped the rain from her eyes. Where was Gabe?

"Gabe, let's go!"

Samir danced back from a wave that hardly broke. It was going on six o'clock but the sun was clouded over.

After she cried out, things happened so fast she didn't know what came first. Maybe Samir turned. Or maybe Gabe showed up beside him. The rain turned blinding.

That's when she heard Gabe yelling at the kid.

"You got no right to be in this place. This is ours. This is *our beach*. This is my friend's beach. Get the fuck out of my sight."

The boy looked confused and didn't move. He had the water behind him and Gabe in front of him. He'd have to step into the water to get past Gabe.

Gabe shoved the boy's chest.

"Are you deaf? Fucking get away from here! Go home."

The boy nearly fell back, and that made him flail toward the surf just before he caught his balance. Then he stumbled around Gabe. And in the stumbling, he shoved Gabe in the belly.

The move was so quick that Olive couldn't tell if he only

reached out to keep from falling into the water and Gabe was a lifeline, or if it was a smooth up yours right back.

On the beach he fled fast as a wild horse. He leaped over trees downed by the tide and rising high water. He tripped and fell. But almost before Gabe turned toward him in rage, the kid was part of the gray trees in the distance.

Gabe was beside Olive. He pressed down on his thighs and gasped for breath like he'd been running, but his eyes looked like he was gasping with anger. He picked up his sweatshirt and tossed it around her shoulders.

"What'd he do to you?" she called into the wind and rain.

Across from them, the horse let out a high-pitched whinny.

Gabe turned and ran from the beach. She caught his T-shirt in her fist. It was cold.

"He invaded us. I hate the sight of him. I know all about him," Gabe shouted. "He's got no business here. They need to move on."

Olive walked after him, not running. She put her cap back on. She lifted the hood of Gabe's sweatshirt over her hair that lay wet on her shoulders.

"Does it have to do with Chris?" she called. "Did he hurt Chris?"

They cut back through the woods to where Gabe had left the dirt bike.

"Yeah, he hurt Chris. Not directly, but that's what people coming across the border do. You want to know how fentanyl gets here? It's all over the web. Mexican cartels are making a fortune off us."

He slammed down the starter of the dirt bike with his

foot. Olive wrapped her hair up high and put on the helmet he kept for her. She climbed on the back of his bike that was screaming.

"Across the border?" Olive yelled over the scream, trying to make sense.

"We got to find some safe place in this country."

4

SAMIR

Samir raced home from the cove on the yellow bike he'd borrowed from his grandfather. He pedaled hard and let his chest thud.

He felt the anger of Gabe's hand on his chest, and he winced. It was two miles to get to the bridge over the river that curved like an S through the city. When he finally got to the parking lot of the River's Tale Café where he worked on the other side, he pulled over. He leaned against a fence, opened his mouth and drew hard on the air. His chest ached.

He wouldn't tell his father what had happened at the cove. He had had the lecture like every Bhutanese Nepali kid who came from the refugee camp. Nepal was very violent in places.

Here in America, the fathers said, *you should not get in fight with anybody. It is not Nepal where you can get away with doing whatever you want. Here you have to obey the rule. We do not bring trouble. If you bring trouble, it will hurt everyone. Your sister. Your mother. No fighting.*

Baba wouldn't be home. He and Samir's uncle had new jobs at Walmart until 11 p.m. many nights. When they were not at Walmart, they were businessmen opening their family's restaurant. He had just helped his father yesterday with the landlord of their new restaurant. That's what was important.

Before they moved to Mersea, Samir lived in Worcester almost four years. Worcester was what he knew about America. Many Bhutanese Nepali families lived there. Here on the New Hampshire Seacoast, just a few. There were the Paudels and Bishnu, Baba's old friend he got kicked out of Bhutan with, and Bishnu's family. That's why his ama said it was in New Hampshire they could make a success with a Nepali restaurant. The only place, his shrewd mom said, to get dumplings. It was Ama who had found the small house in Mersea.

The yellow bike and his heart ground up the hill of Chestnut Street and got him home.

Just then his phone rang. Heera. He didn't want to talk about the cove. Not now.

He took in a large breath. Tried to relax his jaw.

"Hello, Bahini." He opened the gate to his house and Bhim, his little cousin who he called brother, rushed him.

"I've got Heera," he said to Bhim and gave him the phone.

"Hello, little brother. I miss you," Heera said.

Bhim peered into the phone. "Hello, Didi." He called her big sister.

"How is Worcester?" Samir was back on.

"Boring without you."

"Ka garde chau?"

"I'm just doing my homework," she said. "Timi?"

"Me? Same as you." He managed to slow his breath. He flipped his phone and ran inside to the bedroom. He showed her the books and laptop on the mattress he kept beside his grandfather's bed in the daytime.

He dropped his tense body to the mattress.

"Were you dancing?" she said.

"No," he said, "just riding home."

"It's still weird not having you blasting your music and making me dance with you," said Heera.

Bhim dropped on his chest. Samir groaned. Sometimes he would not mind being for just a minute free from interruption. Sometimes he would really like that chance.

"Come to Hajurba." Bhim grabbed Samir's other hand and drew him through the small house to his grandfather and aunt who'd been working in the garden since the rain stopped. Now they were on the narrow front porch.

Auntie sang out to Heera in Nepali. "How is Ama?"

"She is fine," Heera said.

"How is the garden? Bring mustard greens when you come."

"Yes, we will, Auntie."

Samir exhaled long. His grandfather was tired and he settled in a red kitchen chair beside the small wire house for their chickens. Samir brought his hands together and bowed his head.

"Namaskaar, Hajurba," Samir said. "I have Heera."

"I called to say goodnight," Heera said to him in Nepali.

Hajurba said, "Tell Ama to hurry up and finish schooling."

"I am now finishing tenth grade, and Ama finishes in two months."

Hajurba told her that he, too, was studying. He was learning a little English. He had gone to the river with his English class.

"Here people swim in the rivers," he said. "You will swim, too. Samir will teach you when you come."

They all said good night. *Dream of the moon.*

Samir didn't want to think about swimming. He was terrified of the water. And the boy who hated him had put his own body between Samir and land.

Standing in the grass now, he felt his feet solid on the ground. He walked Heera through the tall grass.

"It's because of Hajurama he wants us to learn to swim," Heera said. "Baba says I look like her. Maybe that's because he only knew her when she was young."

Samir didn't want to talk about the river. He wanted to pretend he had not gone there today and would not go again. But then, he didn't like keeping something from her.

"I met a kid tonight," he said quickly. "Don't worry about this, but he wants to fight me. I saw him at the river. Nothing happened. So, now, goodnight. Now you know everything about me like you always do."

"What do you mean? What happened? Do you know his name?"

"Nothing happened. I only know he's a friend of the girl who lives across the street. Good night, Bahini."

"You're okay?"

"All of me. I'm fine. Everyone's fine."

Late that night, Baba and Uncle Tej came home when everybody but Samir was already sleeping. Samir listened to their voices that carried from the porch where Baba and Uncle ate warm tarkari that Baba made. They talked about families still trying to bring their elders from Pathri, the refugee settlement where Samir and Heera were born. They missed the lost hillside in Bhutan, but they also missed Pathri, where their families waited to be allowed to go home to Bhutan.

In New Hampshire, Samir's job was to take care of his grandfather, speak English for everyone but don't forget Nepali. Help Hajurba and Auntie speak English. Never miss work, excel in school. Baba would post pictures of his son and daughter when they earned merit. Help Baba open the business. Keep talking with Heera. Make space in the fall to play soccer. Samir could dance if he wanted. He was a natural dancer. But he could not fight.

Samir was sixteen years old and he wanted to fight. There had been plenty of fights in Nepal. In the villages they were usually with bare fists, knocking a guy down, kicking him. They usually started with something about somebody's girlfriend. The fights got big. So you had fifty boys beating another fifty boys.

Samir had gotten into more than one, even at age eleven years.

In the other room, he heard the men talking. That felt good. With Baba home, he did not worry about Hajurba being alone.

Then his mind went to the girl who lived across the street. She lived in her house alone with her mother. Where was her family? He had heard there was a boy who lived there, who he thought must be her brother. But Samir had never seen him.

He had seen the boy from the cove on her porch. The girl, Olive, had shouted his name.

Gabe.

5

OLIVE

When Olive got home, she and her mom ate supper in the art room.

They ate from bowls mounded with pasta and sauce Mom made with lots of hot pepper flakes — her basic recipe.

"You're shivering," Mom said. "Where've you been?" She tossed Olive a fleece blanket.

"At the cove," Olive said. "Gabe and me."

What happened tonight was all mixed up with Chris. She wouldn't take her mom there.

They settled into what used to be a screened-in porch that Dad and Chris had closed in with pine boards. Dad was a carpenter. They had scavenged the biggest piece of window glass they could find to let light come in. The sun warmed the room in the late afternoon and that was where they lived mostly, and Mom had an easel.

"You didn't text," Mom said.

She forgot. Mom always needed to know when Olive was coming home. Whenever Chris didn't come home that last year, they never knew where he was. If he *would* come home.

"Sorry," she said, barely out loud.

She could almost hear *Crapfire, lighten up*, from her brother.

Her mother had changed from her khaki uniform shirt and pulled on a T-shirt. Her eyes were the same earthy brown as Olive's. Sometimes people thought they were sisters.

Her name was Kathleen, which Olive thought was classy.

Finally, Olive said, "I'm glad you're home."

"You want to talk to me?"

"I always want to."

It was so hard to talk.

Mom was an aide with the therapeutic community in the county jail. She worked with women close to release who were supposed to learn how to manage themselves and how to take care of each other, be responsible. Their arrests were all about drugs.

She took the job after Chris died.

"Are you here tomorrow?" Olive asked.

"God, I hope so. I need a long sleep. I keep meaning to grow something out there." She gestured to the backyard outside the picture window. "But all I want to do is sleep."

"How are things in the TC?"

"They do this discussion therapy. They can talk better if they're making something with their hands, so today I took in yarn and showed them how to cast on, turn a corner. They laughed at the squares they crocheted, then they cried about missing their kids."

Olive wondered if her mom had paid any attention to the people who moved in across the street. Did they ever talk? She tried to not think about the boy.

When she finished eating, Mom sat at the easel sketching on a small piece of card stock attached to the center. The sun had set, but maybe she hadn't noticed the light fading. Her auburn hair was tied in a knot at her neck.

"Now what are you making?"

"A card for Simone's birthday. Irises."

Olive grabbed their bowls and forks. The fleece dropped off one shoulder.

"Once Simone gave me a bunch of irises," Olive said. "She was about two. And when she gave them to me, she burst out crying because she had to give them up."

Mom laughed. "She had white hair when she was born. All the Boudreau kids did."

Olive stood behind Mom and watched the irises turn bright purple. She laid her chin on Mom's shoulder.

"You kids," Mom said, like she was remembering Chris, Gabe and Olive when Mom and Julia were practically kids themselves. She lifted her cup of wine and sipped. She hadn't painted too much since Chris died.

"You hear from Dad lately?" Mom said.

"He's on a job up north," Olive said. "So, no. He's never much good on the phone."

After Dad and Chris built the art room, Dad hung a picture on the wall. There was a knight on a horse. The painter only drew the lines of the man and the horse's body.

Olive had always liked the picture. Maybe Dad had been trying to say knights come in different kinds of ways. But Mom and Dad got divorced when Olive was twelve.

When Chris died, Dad wept in a way that hurt them all to watch. He'd always avoided signs of affection. He was wry and forgetful and needy and devoted in his way and could fix things. Olive wondered if deep down Mom missed him, too.

Mom's phone rang, and she got into a chat with her friend.

"Girl talk," Mom said, waving Olive away.

Olive said, "I'm a girl." She'd like to talk about the way Lord of the Fishes lifted his front legs just for a second when thunder struck, and how a girl's body rises up with hunger for a boy. Her mother understood loving a boy like that, and it might feel sort of like healing for the families when Olive started staying over at Gabe's.

But Mom shooed her away.

Olive sat on the glider swing with Ralph the striped cat and an old Gibson guitar that her father left with her after he moved up north. She had her algebra workbook in her lap. She liked algebra. But she turned the porch light off and watched the street.

Just then the door slammed at the house across the street, and the lady, a man and a little boy appeared. Had that kid Samir gone home?

She moved to the table in the corner where she and Chris used to eat bagels on summer mornings. They got sesame seeds all the heck over the place. She was slipping into a dark place where everything about her house killed her.

She called Lise, her best friend.

"Hey," Lise said.

Lise wore a band of aqua-blue eyeliner that came to a perfect arc at the edge of her eyes. She called herself a political poet.

"Is the whole algebra packet due tomorrow?" Olive asked.

"You want to talk about algebra?"

"I want to talk about normal things."

Across the street Olive could hear the neighbor's hoe hitting stones in the garden. *Chink. Chink.* She heard the song from *The Hunger Games* coming through Lise's phone. Chris was twelve when they saw that movie. Olive was ten.

"What's going on?" Lise said.

"It's June."

Olive thought Samir's house was like a sucker tree that sprouted up between the regular ones. Was the boy going to come out next? It was almost too dim to see.

"The neighbors are out," she whispered.

"You mean the boy. What's his name?"

"Samir, yeah. Gabe said he bet those people never lived in a truck like he did."

"Gabe was homeless?"

"Yeah. When he was little they got evicted from their apartment in Dover." She turned and dropped on her belly at the far end of the porch. That way she felt like it was just her and Lise. "Later they got the house."

She watched the people across the street and heard the hum of their voices. She felt rage at the sound of them. These people were disruptive in the neighborhood.

Lise turned her music off. "Did something happen?"

"Why do people hate each other so much?"

"I hate so many people," Lise said.

"I mean in-your-face hate. Like if you don't even know somebody and you hate them."

"Like racists?"

"I don't know," Olive said. "You're the political poet. What is a political poet?"

"They hold people accountable. Like about rapists who get away with it."

"Sometimes I feel like I hate somebody, when I really hate something else."

"You're the only person I currently don't hate," Lise said. Then she said, "So what'd Gabe do?"

"Gabe hates that boy. We saw him this afternoon at the cove."

A scream came from the street. A fox or a fisher cat from the woods near the creek.

"He screamed at him like those fisher cats."

"For what?"

"For being here."

Lise sighed. "Gabe's different. Everybody's different since last summer. Gabe calls me a socialist. That's the worst word he can think of." She laughed.

"He likes you," Olive said.

"I like him, too. He's just different since last summer."

"You're political. I don't think I think that way. I mean, your ideas are big. And you know where you stand and who's good and who's bad. Like, you know you're a socialist. I don't know what I am."

"My dad went to marches for peace. Marches for Black Lives Matter. Marches for rent reduction."

"I can't imagine having that dad." Olive rolled on her back and looked at the sky. "We used to have flowers all around that Mom grew, remember? We used to have this wild and rangy garden like us kids."

"If you start to relive things," Lise said. "Come over here." She was talking about Chris.

Olive didn't answer. All she knew at this moment was that her whole body was taking in the smell of the lilac and honeysuckle that infiltrated her porch from the neighbor's bushes beside their broken-down fence.

6

SAMIR

The River's Tale Café was not much bigger than Samir's house. Inside, everything happened loud and fast. Behind the café was a creek that wound through the village and fed the river a few miles beyond and finally the Atlantic Ocean. Samir liked the white trees that grew at an angle out of the creek bank.

He still felt both worry and wonder that last January when they arrived, the owner, Ethel, had given him the early-morning dishwashing job.

Now at six in the morning on Monday in the last week of school, the sign flashed at the café. *Breakfast. Lunch.* Purple lilacs bloomed on the path. The leaves on the birch trees were bright green and flipped in the wind.

On weekends he worked until noon. On school days

he did morning opening, swept out the booths, filled up the sugar, salt, pepper and napkins bins. Emptied the dishwasher, bused tables, loaded the dishwasher and ran it before he left for school at 7:45.

He knew Ethel would serve breakfast until 10:30. Don't even ask after that.

Inside, a table of workmen laughed loudly. Ethel refilled their coffee that they whitened with cream.

Samir worked fast. She'd expect him to stay late if something wasn't done. He had piled up plates for the cook to easily reach, he stacked mugs on the shelf beneath the coffee maker. He'd bus the current tables, load the dishes.

Just then — it was already 7:30 — the boy shoved open the café door. The boy from the cove.

Samir felt his stomach tighten and drop and then the pang in the side of his head. He had been holding a tray of dirty plates, and he froze with the plates precariously still.

When Gabe saw him, his face opened in surprise. Samir realized Gabe didn't know Samir worked here. He watched Gabe rest his hands low on his hips.

"Got your peaches, Ethel," Gabe shouted. He didn't take his eyes off Samir. Samir stood still with the stack of white plates.

Ethel put down the coffee pot and grabbed the large box Gabe carried. It had perfect circles of fruits painted on its sides.

"Your mom's a peach," Ethel said. She spoke very loudly. Everything she said was loud, and Gabe had to turn to her.

With a knife, they loosened the lid of the box and opened it. The smell of fresh peaches wafted into the café.

"Mom got twice this much. She loves when the peaches come ripe on my grandfather's farm."

"Ah, yeah, she's a Georgia girl, your mom."

"She knew you could use them," Gabe said, "so here you go."

Ethel had her hair tied up on her head and wore a short fitted, floral dress. She was compact and dressed for movement and work.

"Sure can," she said and began to build a display of peaches, mounding them deftly in a metal bowl and then built a little mountain of peaches. "Peach cobbler special. We'll put it on Facebook. Summer's here, folks. Fresh peaches direct from Georgia."

Samir's and Gabe's eyes flashed to each other while they both waited for the crash of all those peaches.

"Hey, kid," the short-order cook called. "You got another use for those plates than to get 'em in the washer for the next breakfasts?"

Samir jolted into action. He turned to load the plates in the back kitchen. Then returned to the front because there were more tables to bus.

Another guy walked in. He looked like a small hot-air balloon and was older than Gabe. He and Gabe slapped each other on the back like American men sometimes did. The older man wore a reflective vest and a red baseball cap. At the doorstep he had a fit of coughing.

Finally he called out to Ethel, "Hey, my girl, how's it going?"

"Well, Kyle. Haven't seen you in donkey's years. You better see about that cough."

It was 7:40. Samir needed to get out of here. Clear this table, get his jacket and pack. He cleared the table. Loaded the dishes.

"Give 'em coffee," Ethel ordered Samir and motioned to Gabe and the man who had taken a booth.

Samir shook his head. He did not want to give them coffee. He had taken off his River's Tale apron. He motioned to the door.

"I have school," he said to Ethel.

"Just get the *coffee!*" she commanded. "What is so hard about giving paying customers a cup of coffee? You're working in a restaurant. We don't give people their coffee, we don't make a dime. We're out on the streets. You ever been on the streets? Give 'em a cup of coffee."

Ethel did not wait to hear if Samir had ever been on the streets. That's the language his father used when he talked about getting kicked out of Bhutan. When he was Samir's age, he tried to stay in India where they were illegal and lived on the streets in Bhagalpur. His parents in Bhutan did not know if he was alive or dead.

In the River's Tale, Samir understood that Ethel was not offering to have a discussion with him about living on the street. He also knew he could not go home and tell his father he got fired because he didn't bring coffee to Gabe. He would have to tell him who Gabe was and what Gabe did. He would have to show his fear.

Nor did he want to tell his father that he was late for school. Samir was a trusted student. He was supposed to meet with the dance team. At this moment, students were waiting for him in the gym.

The older man had a square face and solemn eyes showing only slits of blue. But his mouth exploded with laughter and coughs as he watched Samir cave to the small woman. The man took off his cap. His hair was sandy, too, though flattened to his head. Samir glanced at Gabe who was pressed into the corner of the booth. He had earbuds in, and he was trying to ignore where he was. But the older man was talking to him.

And then Samir realized this man was probably Gabe's father.

Just get out of here! Samir told himself. He tossed his apron over his shoulder. He filled two thick mugs with black coffee. He slid them on the men's table.

"Got a way with words, Ethel," the father called to her. "You ought to run for school board. Get the federal government out of the schools. Like this kid. Feds probably brought him here."

"I need workers," Ethel hollered from the kitchen. She delivered three plates balanced on her arm. They were stacked with pancakes and hash browns and bacon.

"What are you, Honduran?" the father asked Samir. "The Texans send Hondurans on buses up here to New England. You come by bus?"

Samir ignored him. He was almost out the door. But he could not help stealing one more glance at Gabe. His father elbowed him and Gabe pulled out one earbud. Gabe had pressed his cap down over his eyes. He did not want to listen to his father. Was he embarrassed? Was he afraid? Samir respected his father above all people, and he did not expect to feel emotion for the boy who tried to shove him into the water.

He and Gabe locked eyes for just a second. Did Gabe see in Samir's eyes something he despised? Interest, sympathy, pity?

Gabe's eyes transformed, and for just a second his eyes filled with rage.

Samir thought, *If you don't have your father to respect, what do you have?*

Ethel was still working on the peach display so she could get a photo of the summer colors. They were pale yellows and bright yellows. She made a small mountain to advertise the peach cobbler she would make. She did this, not bending her manicured nails which were dark red like Ama's.

Samir knew yellow was the color of the third chakra. Hajurba had taught Samir to imagine a yellow ball between his palms.

Breathe into it, he had said. *Let the fire of your breath blow up the yellow ball. Then feel the yellow ball build fire in you.*

In me? he had asked when he was small. *How does it get in me?*

I don't know, Hajurba had said. *It just gets inside your body. Breathe to make it hot. In this way you lose your suffering.*

"What is suffering?" Samir had asked.

"Missing someone," Hajurba said.

When Ethel was done, she stepped back and away from the display. Her stepping back gave Samir a path to the door. As he passed, his backpack lightly touched a single peach.

First one peach, then a river of peaches loosened and fell to the old wood floor. Samir was delayed again because he stooped to the ground and gathered each of the peaches one by one. He mounded them again in the bowl and arranged more peaches in a way that would be beautiful for the River's Tale Café Facebook page.

He didn't look at Ethel. She had been hurling a string of curses. She gave up while he worked and slid plates of omelets off the shelf and took them to people. She didn't look at Samir again. Samir rebuilt the mountain, strategically, swiftly.

He told Ethel, "I'll see you tomorrow," only to confirm that he wasn't fired. He pushed open the door and was glad to see the birch trees again.

He was about to step out when Gabe appeared behind him. Samir turned to hear the pound of the bottom of Gabe's boot as he kicked the display of peaches. The peaches flew, and there was a thunder roll of peaches as they hit the ground. Samir felt the boy's hate of him.

Now Samir watched the peaches still rolling down the center of the café. He thought Gabe's father would shout at him. But he didn't. His father grabbed for the peaches and laughed.

There will always be Gabes. That is what Baba would say. Take it easy. You're going to do better in life than a bully. But Samir was insulted and wanted revenge. He was also afraid.

7

OLIVE

On Monday evening, Gabe screeched up the driveway in his dilapidated Prius.

He got the car when somebody was selling a Prius with 200,000 miles for a song on Craigslist. He saw it basically needed a battery, knew it was a deal. "What the fuck is that?" Kyle had said. "Old Prius," Gabe said. Olive thought he was making a point that he wasn't like his dad at all.

Now Gabe came tearing up the porch steps stinking like the sweat-drenched dirt-bike gear that lived in his car. Olive wrapped him in her sweater sleeves. Nero leapt up the steps and she wrapped him and his floppy ears in there, too. Gabe had her in his arms. Then he fetched supplies from the Prius trunk that smelled even stronger than dirt-bike sweat.

"Where's your mom?" He spun Olive around with a long loaf of bread over their heads. "I'm cooking."

"She's going to be late. If it weren't for you," Olive said, "we'd die of spaghetti." She pulled the loaf of warm crusty bread from the bag as she opened the screen door, ripped off a hunk.

Before long he had the kitchen torn apart and the whole house smelled like garlic and basil churning in the blender with Parmesan cheese he liked to get in a block and grate himself. He was a creative guy.

In the middle of things, Olive put her hands on his hips and kissed his straight lips. His eyes were jumpy. He was tired. But she loved when the kitchen was full of his energy. They cooked up pesto pizza on the crusty bread and heaped it with tomatoes. The pesto was brilliant green and shiny with oil. Both Mom and Olive knew their food was ordinary compared to what Gabe could throw together.

They sat on the porch stoop and waited for Mom, who had texted again. "Soon." They got up and danced. No music. They held each other and swayed.

"You ever dream?" Gabe said softly.

"On a night like this, I can hear Chris singing in the shower. I don't have to be dreaming to hear it. He's as real as you, Gabe." She put her hand flat on his chest.

He dipped her and she laughed when he scooped her up.

"I have this dream for us," he said. "I'll buy us some land. Build properties. I've been reading about business management. I'm looking at math classes at the college."

"Might take a while," Olive said.

"Will you come?"

"You mean, will I take this boy?"

"Yeah, like that," he said.

"I take this boy," she said.

"I take you."

"I think we just got married."

"Yup."

Olive said, "I dream. I want to become something." What were the words for what she was imagining? The night had gotten quieter. "I want to become someone who rides horses." She laughed. "I don't know why I said that. I just remember Lord of the Fishes on the island. I've never ridden a horse. Maybe it's like flying and you can feel his huge heartbeat."

"You're a nerdy kid," he said and kissed her. "I don't know if I have any better chance than my dad." Gabe's voice grew deep and quiet. "Sometimes I can't get out. Like there's walls everywhere. Like there's nowhere to go. That's where that kid comes in."

He was talking about the kid across the street.

"I didn't get this till after Chris died. It was hard as hell getting treatment for him. But afterward I read up on why. The country is changing. Now they support people coming across the borders. That's where the money's going. There's nothing for treatment for white boys who don't have a dime. Or there are strings attached, like you have to have insurance to pay for in-house treatment."

He was talking softly like he wanted her to understand.

"Fentanyl killed Chris. Fentanyl's a synthetic and you know where they make it? Labs in Mexico. It comes from Mexicans crossing the border. They say there's no such thing as long-term fentanyl use. They all die. And immigrants are making big bucks."

He had said that about Mexicans that night at the cove. He put his mouth in her hair.

His eyes were gray in the dark. They almost pinned her to the swing. He kissed her and she felt it like a charge that began at her bare feet and lifted her.

"I keep seeing that kid." Gabe's jaw turned stony. "I want you to understand. What I was telling him is, don't fuck with me, with you, our family, the way people fucked with my friend. This country didn't help Chris. This country doesn't care about us. The rights of minorities are what matter here. We have to take care of each other."

She thought about Kyle's sign — *Keep New England White*.

Gabe said, "It was a warning. I don't want any of 'em here. Did you know he works at the River's Tale? Kyle and I saw him this morning. We were goofing with the kid. He needs to know he's got no future here."

"Because my brother died."

"He didn't need to die, Olive. No one helped him. And all those guys at the Yard. There's a steady stream of foreigners to take their place." She knew Gabe's dad lost his job at the Navy Yard. But he was a drinker and that didn't help. "Pretty soon, even in New Hampshire, we're going to be strangers."

"You saw your dad today," she said.

"Like I said, just breakfast." He looked at her funny, like she might have proof of more, but Olive thought that was about him and Kyle and their hard relationship. Gabe and Simone had a lot of Kyle stories. The time Kyle broke in through the bathroom window 'cause Julia locked the front door on him. Kyle was drunk sometimes.

Olive thought about her mom's job at the county jail. It was a jail where ICE detained illegals they picked up in sweeps. Mom said people came to pray for them. Protesters had held a Walk for Immigrants march from Boston. They came to the jail and held hands in a circle and carried bright streamers and sang "Would You Harbor Me?" She said the inmates she knew were pissed since they were white people who got into drugs.

"Do you have to be illegal for somebody to pray for you?" That's what Gabe said.

"I'm fishing early," he said. "Gotta go soon."

They went in the kitchen, grabbed up slices of the thick pizza, leaning into the counter, facing each other, and they ate and it almost felt like they were one person. Olive felt full just watching him bang down three slices in a row.

She packed up more for him to take on the boat for the middle of the night when he motored into the sea.

Olive sat alone on the porch with the cat.

She glanced across the street. The woman and Samir came out of their house on a blast of music. Light streamed from their porch onto the yard. Olive looked through the trees and saw the woman bend to the garden.

Samir was in a white shirt dancing across where the dandelion puffballs used to be.

Then a voice called out from inside the red bungalow. Samir ran up the creaking steps past their hen who laid pale green eggs, which Olive knew about because that hen had laid a single egg under her own chestnut tree. They had stupid chickens, too, that they let run free.

Samir opened his door full wide with a high side kick. Who was this dude?

Olive shouted, "We're calling the police, you don't turn that racket down."

Mom came home, and she went inside to eat Gabe's beautiful pesto pizza. Mom was really tired and soon went upstairs to her bedroom.

Olive crept back outside and stretched out on the glider. The foreigners had gone indoors, the street was quiet. Ralph the cat's muzzle rested on Olive's throat. He curled beside her shoulder and snored. The Day Night Store calmed down. People stopped blasting their horns at drivers for blocking the pump while they ambled in for coffee and a donut — $1.29 all-night special.

Then, quietly, out came Samir. Next came the old man. The man sat on a yellow couch they used like lawn furniture. The porch railing was a skinny table. A rusted yellow bike leaned on the side of the porch.

Samir brought the old man a round plate that glinted. He set it on the railing. The old man ate from the plate quickly with his fingers. Samir sat beside him and ate, too.

The cat jumped into the dark. Olive stretched out on her belly and watched like they were a movie. The glider creaked and the wind blew and kept bending the chestnut tree. The boy collected their plates, cups and the pot. He took them inside and came back with a basin. The old man put his feet, which must have been bare, right there in the basin.

On the porch Olive jumped off the swing. It rammed into the wall with a thud. Samir shouted, "Go inside. Hajurba, go." Then the people who'd come to invade their city went into their house, and the only sound was the high-pitched voice from the lady in the language Olive didn't know.

And you know what the kid did next? He cranked the music. Bollywood music. It blasted from a big-screen TV she could see inside his porch window. He leapt out the door. He was doing the moves of the dancer in the Bollywood song. He raced across the dandelions and weeds and the lobster traps the fisherman left behind.

For a fleeting second, all she could see was the grace of his moves.

8

SAMIR

"Ka garde chau?" Heera sang out.

Samir propped the phone up against a pitcher and talked while he stuffed dumplings in his mouth.

"Not much. Timi?"

"You're so closed off. Tell me what's going on," she said.

"There's a girl across the street. I don't know much else about her."

"A special girl?"

"No! Just a girl."

"Did something happen?"

Heera was in his old kitchen. Behind her, the teapot was on the white stove like always. It was scarred with dings and chips like an old man's face. That is where they always left the teapot after Hajurba lit the burner and boiled the water.

He could see her smearing jelly on bread. He didn't answer right away, and she held up the phone to look at him with his face stuffed with momo.

"What happened to your eye?" A purple bruise splotched across his forehead, but he had not paid attention. He touched his head as if he could hide it.

"Oh, I fell. I was down at the cove with Hajurba. There's a bunch of dead trees across the sand."

"You fell over the trees?"

"I was looking at the water." That was not untrue.

She looked suspicious, but bit into her jelly bread.

"What about the girl? Do you see that boy who wants to fight? You said he hangs out with her."

"She sings," he said.

He would talk about the girl. But he didn't want to talk about Gabe. Or the peaches. Those were the kinds of insults Heera knew.

"I can hear her sometimes in the night," Samir said.

Then he thought of his grandfather who sang love songs on their own porch. It was when he got lost in his memories and there was a sadness in him.

Samir told Heera, "She has a pretty good voice. I think her parents are divorced. At school I heard her talk about her brother but I haven't seen him."

"They don't talk to you?" Anger flickered across her eyes, and her lips pouted like their ama's did sometimes.

"I don't talk to them. Neither of us talk," Samir said. "I go to work very early at the café."

He held up the apron he had to bring home to wash with the three purple fishes across the hip.

"We are fine," he said. "Everything is great here and you'll like it when you come."

"I already like it. I want to see what it's like in June. You're not far, but we are so busy!"

"I have to prepare for our last class. You, Bahini, go do your homework." Then he slipped because he missed her so much. "We both knew in America we'd be in a place with a bunch of white people."

"What is the matter with you?"

"Nothing. It's just easier when you're with your own people. So if somebody messes with you in Worcester, like checking your money to make sure it's real, or pretending you don't exist, we just all stay together and you're okay." That was all that was the matter.

"Good. So now I am coming. We'll be together."

After he hung up, he allowed himself to feel lonely. He had had three friends in the refugee camp at Pathri who were all dancers like him. These three friends came to the US, but they'd gone to different states. He allowed himself to miss them. They were just kids, but they all taught themselves to dance with videos. Then they watched each other.

Samir clicked on some Nepali rappers whose music made him feel less alone. He liked Yama Buddha okay but others more.

His English teacher, Mr. Wyeth, had said he could include Nepali in a poem. Students were reading a poem or giving some kind of presentation on the last day of school. Samir thought about singing "Saathi," Yama Buddha's rap about his best friend who died from drugs. He wanted to give Mr. Wyeth a translation so he could make sense of it, and he'd found the Nepali written in Roman script. This could seal his good grade.

From Samir's phone Yama Buddha sang.

Ta ra ma daju bhai jasari bachinthyo …
You and I would have lived like brothers …
Tara saathi nikai nai eklo chu aile …
However, I really am lonely this day, my friend …

The song made him too sad to sing for his class. The other students would make fun of him. He could read his essay about home. "I was born in Pathri in Eastern Nepal. I lived in the refugee camp. My family was deported from Bhutan before I was born." He could add *at gunpoint.* "I lived in Pathri until I was eleven years."

No. They would fall asleep.

He'd perform. He would write a rap. It wasn't as good as dancing, but he could do it well.

He had to move, he had to dance to get out of his head. He needed lots and lots and lots of space to dance and feel the space in his body.

He danced out the door. There was a path along tall pine trees between his house and the main road. He ran and leaped over pine needles. The smell was warm and sweet. He liked these tall pine trees. There were many, many houses in their Creek Village with paths among them. And that's where he danced, on the paths with the trees. His teacher had watched him dance in the school gym and he proclaimed that he danced "with joy and careless abandon." Samir smiled as he danced — the hip bumps, the sway, the swirl through the pine needles, his palms opening the world for himself.

What if New Hampshire was full of Gabe Boudreaus?

Samir plotted the ways to fight back and, as he danced, he wanted to explode that yellow ball.

9

OLIVE

Lise Landerman had tattoos on her forearms. They were fake but new, so they looked almost real. One was a black lace sleeve. Olive's favorite was the other one, a little monster from *Where the Wild Things Are* with human feet and claws for fingers. Lise wore one earring with a chain tassel that grazed her shoulder. Olive wore Chris's canvas jacket.

They met in the woods by the creek. They sat with their backs to a giant pine tree while they hunted for jobs on their phones.

Olive said, "My mom's still working with women at the jail. Sometimes I pretend my brother's in the men's unit. Like he got arrested and they sentenced him to rehab at the county jail."

"Like the guy that got arrested at the Rite Aid," Lise said.

The cops had to break into the bathroom at Rite Aid where a man barricaded himself after he tried to hold up the store for drugs. They locked the doors and people stood outside in the parking lot. They could hear him wailing as they took him out through the back. It was an awful sound.

But then the man was sent to the county jail. Maybe he was there right now getting a haircut in a room the size of a closet. Maybe with counseling and medical care, being arrested would have given Chris a second chance.

"Look," Lise said.

Olive looked down the path where she pointed. Someone was in the distance.

Lise said, "He probably thinks he's all alone in the woods."

Sure enough, it was the boy Gabe wanted gone.

He was dancing. She could see the movement between the light and the tree trunks.

"Look at him." Lise laughed. "It's like he's dancing on air."

"Geez, he's everywhere."

"You don't like him?"

"I don't know anything about him, personally."

She went back to scrolling job postings. Samir danced.

"The rec center day camp needs counselors," Olive said.

"A girl in the dance club said they really like him." Lise was watching Samir, and Olive caught glimpses of him, too, as he danced almost out of sight now. She saw him through Gabe's eyes. She saw the problems for people who'd always lived in a place when immigrants moved in. Samir's family probably had health care, and maybe jobs that a lot of people born here didn't have. So no wonder people complained about them.

"Why don't you like him?" Lise asked.

"Things feel weirder since what happened at the cove. He annoys me. Maybe I'm not political and I don't get it."

"Maybe I'm not political, either," Lise said. "Maybe I just hate people with power who get away with whatever they want. People who make policies that hurt other people."

People with the power to decide if her brother would die. Olive thought of what Gabe said. Was that what Gabe was doing? Naming the ones who hurt Chris?

10

SAMIR

At dawn, Auntie and Uncle were still asleep in the small back bedroom. Samir used to sleep on a mattress in Hajurba's room, but Bhim didn't like being alone where he slept on the couch in the living room. They often, then, brought the mattress to the living room so Samir could keep him company.

In the daytime, the mattress was Samir's getaway place to study, back by Hajurba's bed.

Hajurba was praying at the shrine in his room like always, sitting in the Buddha position. Samir stepped over his grand-father in the early light, dressed, gathered his pack and went to the kitchen.

Baba was making tea. The calls of birds came through the open back door. In the kitchen garden, vegetables were sprouting. Leaves would be ready to dry in the sun to make gundruk, and they could cook soup with the leaves when the restaurant opened. Baba had cleared away tree branches to let the sun in, and now herbs covered all the backyard. When the tea was prepared, they both drank from cups with the picture of the famous purple finch of New Hampshire.

A truck ground its way up Chestnut Street. Baba computed numbers on his phone and scratched notes on a pad.

"Ama would be making sel roti," Samir said.

"Yes," Baba said, distracted.

Samir missed Ama's cooking. In a few minutes he'd go to work and smell bacon frying and bitter coffee. He hunched over his tea and liked these few minutes with his father.

At that very moment, with the hot tea in his mouth, a rattling thud shook the kitchen window. The sound straightened Samir, and he felt it up his spine. He gulped the tea in his mouth.

Another thud. Then a cracking.

In one leap Baba was at the open kitchen door. Samir was beside him.

They didn't see anyone. Baba walked around the garden patch to a thicket of limbs and birches and sprawling thorny shrubs. From the thicket came the sounds of the street beyond. But when Samir's eyes adjusted to the dim light, he saw movement through the thicket as someone moved, too far away to see.

"Where is he now?" Baba's voice was sharp and tense. "Is he still here? This is a funny trick?" He picked up a reddish brick on the ground outside the kitchen window. Then another.

They were new bricks from a place where someone was building a new wall or a walkway.

Inside, Baba lifted his hands to the window. His face was seared with anger. Whoever it was had not thrown the brick accurately or fast enough to shatter the glass. But they had cracked the glass corner to corner. There were many starbursts and the window would now easily shatter.

Baba's voice broke through the house. "Doesn't this person have something better to do? What kind of person would do this? If it's a child, what kind of parents would allow a child to throw bricks? I would never allow a child of mine to do this."

"I'll go after him." Samir was out the door.

"You will not!" Baba said. Samir stopped.

When the Paudels first moved in and people did not say hello, Baba always said, "We will stay out of their way, and they will be happy. We will be good neighbors."

This time Baba asked, "Do your aunt and grandfather have more English classes?"

"One more."

"Walk with them when they go. You have to watch them."

"We should make a report to the police," Samir said.

"You don't have to tell me this," Baba said. He knew. Samir watched him punch in the numbers 911. He had never called this number before, and Samir knew he did not want to. He worried about his English, but he spoke into the phone.

"Hello, there is attack on my house."

Samir could not hear the reply, only Baba who said, "Just now. Someone threw brick on my window."

They must have asked for more information. Baba gave his phone number and their address and spelled his full name. He said he did not know who the attacker was. He did not have a description. He told the person he himself was a businessman. Samir knew Baba would hand him the phone if he thought the person he was talking to didn't understand him. But he didn't.

Baba hung up.

Samir grabbed his apron. "Are the police coming?"

"I don't know."

"I'm late, Baba. Let's talk when we both come home."

"We are lucky. The loan is going through. This is the hard time in a new place."

Samir was glad Ama wasn't here now for the hard time.

Baba let out a nervous laugh. He did not look in Samir's eyes.

Samir ran down the porch steps and toward the River's Tale with his fist tight around the wadded apron.

His family did not deserve bricks thrown at their home.

As he ran, his family's stories washed through him.

Bhutanese soldiers arrested Hajurba at the market beside his horse still loaded with cardamom he'd come to sell. They praised the horse because even if they beat Hajurba too much, the horse found his way home to his wife.

And here, what had happened? Their window was cracked corner to corner with explosions in the glass. They were not wanted.

Samir's chest was tight with worry and anger.

When Samir got to the River's Tale, he ran up the steps, half expecting Gabe to be there. He would be by the counter, standing wide-legged in his tight jeans and T-shirt. Samir remembered the brawls with gangs between two schools. In Nepal in a big mud field they'd try to take each other down. Kick to the groin. Vicious jab to the belly.

Samir was worked up by the time he danced across the deck. In the early morning, with no one to see him, he threw jabs in the air. Jab. Jab. Cross to the face. Jab. Jab. Cross to eyeball. Till he came up right to Ethel in the open doorway, and behind her, there wasn't anybody.

11

OLIVE

Mr. Wyeth had a round, rugged, Eeyore sort of face, and when he read to the students, sometimes he cried. He scrunched up his eyes whenever Olive gave him a poem. They were all about Chris.

This class was a lot of poetry. If your counselor recommended you take a class because you liked poems, Mr. Wyeth always let that person in. Samir was recommended even though he didn't always know what people were saying and didn't pronounce some things right. That's how it came to be that Olive had to see Samir at school, even though she ignored him across the street.

Then her mind flashed to her mom. Tonight she had to talk to Mom. She'd started packing, imagining what it would be like to not have to say goodnight to Gabe. They could actually sleep together and wake up together. They'd spent overnights and both their families thought of them as together. They'd both have jobs this summer. That's all they wanted, wasn't it? To be together.

Then Mr. Wyeth's voice snapped her into the classroom. He was reading a poem about the alchemy of a butterfly that could change from a chrysalis to a monarch. Or a flying fish.

Olive was fascinated. What did he mean, a flying fish? She listened to his voice and held on to the words in her mind.

Mr. Wyeth read, "If the butterfly transmogrifies/does it turn into a flying fish?"

At home, she dropped her pack, went to the bathroom and stood in front of the mirror. She felt her hands shake.

She began to brush out her hair. Her hair was dark, almost auburn like Mom's. Gabe liked to hold her hair back from her eyes and give her butterfly kisses.

Her brother was dead. She wanted to be a family with Gabe. She heard Mr. Wyeth's voice. He had paraphrased after he read it. *Can a butterfly's soul travel and become a flying fish?*

A flying horse? A piece of sky? Where did her brother's soul travel to?

Then she saw Chris in the mirror, watching her. Amused.

She opened the linen cupboard and grabbed a pair of scissors.

She began to cut her hair over the bathroom sink. The scissors weren't that sharp. The cuts were ragged. She slowed down and took the hair layer by layer, working slowly. Large chunks of hair dropped on the bath mat, into the tub, all around.

She touched the back of her head. She could feel the tendons in her neck. She picked up the scissors again and cut layers on the top. She touched her cheekbones and her lips. Her eyes were big without all that hair. She was a face with eyes.

She oiled her hair up. Then she pressed white hair-paint wax through it, section by section.

Chris was still there in the bathroom mirror. He was reading to her like he did when she was little and he'd read to her about a horse. She had gone still and listened with her mouth open, one hand folded on the other, her face against her fingers. Mom had a photo. Chris had brown droopy eyes and the little twist of his lips.

In the bathroom, he looked up from the book and said her hair was wicked cool. Her auburn hair was now spirals of white, and on the bottom part at the back of her neck she swirled in some orange.

You got that Jeremy Zucker look going, Chris said.

She kept spinning the orange wax between her fingers, trying to figure out how Chris could just appear like he did.

Thank you, she whispered. She looked back in the mirror, but now it was just her.

She looked like an animal-girl — bones and eyes and tendons and skin. Transmogrified.

Olive scrounged around the kitchen. They had hamburger meat. She used to make this thing called cheesy hamburger and pasta. She just needed cheese. She'd make dinner and then she and Mom could talk.

She opened the door to the world in her new hair. She could feel the afternoon sun on her ears. Amazing! She felt like no one would know who she was.

At the Day Night, Olive bought the cheese. She trudged back up the hill. It was a hard hill to bicycle and sometimes she had to zigzag to get back up it. Today she wanted to walk.

She approached her house, and across the street she saw the neighbors out there trying to mow the grass, but the mower only clicked and didn't turn over.

The old man looked like a flyer in a brown jacket with epaulets. He turned away from the mower. The woman adjusted the tie on her sari and bent to unscrew the gas cap. Samir kicked grass from his sneakers.

Olive and her mom had a push mower that clank-clanked across the grass.

Olive slammed open the garage door, rolled the mower out to the sidewalk and pulled it behind her across the street.

The people stopped and stared at her. For one, her hair was gone and what remained was white with orange fringe. Two, she had never crossed the street to their house before.

"This works," she said. They began talking in excitement in that language. The woman didn't smile but nodded her head.

"You just push it," Olive told Samir, who stood with his hands on his hips far away, his face annoyed and sweaty.

"We didn't have a lawn in Worcester," he muttered.

She pushed the mower to mow a few feet of grass, in case they didn't understand. She left it and strode back across the street.

Samir approached the mower. He had a graceful, rolling gait. He pushed it. The mower clanked along.

The woman called out to Samir and held up her phone to snap him, the mower and the bright green grass.

Olive stopped and turned.

"Bring it back when you're done," she called, so they didn't think she was giving it to them.

In the kitchen, Olive started to fix the cheesy hamburger dish. The boy's easy walk stuck in her mind, and she wondered where he had learned to dance.

The front door opened, and she heard Mom's footsteps.

"I'm making dinner," Olive called. Mom disappeared upstairs.

The kitchen was warm. Olive wiped sweat off her face and tried to push her hair away but there were just sticks of it.

She yelled, "Dinner," at the bottom of the stairs.

Mom appeared, a flash of light in a summer dress. She placed her hands on Olive's cheekbones.

"Your hair."

"I cut it myself."

"I saw." Mom held her face. "Aren't you beautiful," she said, sliding her hands from Olive's cheeks to her sprouts of hair.

They took plates to the little table on the porch and started in on the casserole. It was nothing like eating at Gabe's with all the life and dog and owls and chickens and orioles. They were at the far end of the porch where a thin forsythia tree sprawled over the railing.

"Gabe and I are planning on spending weekends together over the summer," Olive said. "I mean, not here."

"I know," Mom said. "Just finish school."

"I am going to finish school."

"Things happen."

"Mom ... we're not idiots."

"If you're both working and building a life, education gets shoved in the cracks. Don't do that. I did that."

"You're smart like you are." But Olive knew not doing all her college nagged at Mom. Her *if only.*

Mom pressed the back of her hand to her mouth. Her long hair fell over her left eye.

Mom got up. Olive, too. They stacked the plates and headed in and Olive knew she was going to Gabe's like she wanted to. That was the path they were all on.

Mom got out her phone.

"Holy shit," Mom said. "Somebody's saying there was vandalism at a Chestnut Street house. Somebody threw a brick into a kitchen window."

"Like here?"

"They're looking to talk to anybody with information. Jeez. Says it was 170 Chestnut."

The Ronans were 175.

"That's across the street," Olive said.

"Must have been a dare, kids on a summer night daring each other." But Mom and Olive went around and locked the windows and the doors. They kept checking for more information, but nobody knew.

When Mom went upstairs, Olive wondered about the place where her lawn mower was. Were the people over there scared in the dark?

She went out to sit on the glider swing and called Gabe. "Let's meet at the cemetery."

"Early work. Tomorrow?"

"Can you hear the owls?"

"Yes."

"I can't sleep."

"What are you wearing?"

She went inside to the art room where she closed the door and swayed in the dark. "Nothing. Gabriel, rock me."

"What's the matter?"

"You know those people across the street?"

"Yeah."

"Somebody threw bricks at their window. It feels weird here. Mom and I were creeping around with the lights off, making sure the locks worked."

"You're okay. It's just that people don't like them. They're trouble. You can already feel it."

"I wish this would all go away."

"You talk to your mom?"

"Yeah, it's fine. We're fine. Gabe, Mom made us lock all the windows."

12

SAMIR

It was the last day of school. Samir had not lost his job. Beginning tomorrow he could work from 6 a.m. until 2 p.m. Baba said this was very good, because he would observe how Ethel ran the café. Samir would learn some of the tricks of American business.

Mr. Wyeth had arranged the students' desks in a crooked circle. He had laid out donuts that Samir knew Ethel sold at the River's Tale — raspberry, blueberry and iced with maple frosting. He had carried heavy trays of these sweets to the display case at the café.

In this circle he would perform his poem.

Samir glanced at Mr. Wyeth, who sat hunched in the sunlight. Azaleas bloomed through the window behind him, which Samir knew as the national flower of Nepal. One by one each student came to the front to read.

The girl Olive stood. But she had cut her hair. She had cut it not just up to her shoulders as he had seen Heera cut her hair. The girl across the street had cut her hair close to her head. Also, it was white. She looked like a boy.

Mr. Wyeth watched her, too. He had worry in his eyes, but he often had worried eyes. Samir looked down, but then back up at this girl who was reading a poem. He had not followed the poem. He was worried about her hair.

Samir's mother and Heera, his aunt Geeta, his family still in Nepal — all had long hair. Some elders in his family would say if a young woman cut her hair short, she was acting like a man. Here Samir knew lots of girls with short hair, but he thought Olive's long dark hair was becoming.

She had brown eyes and he would also use the word delving. She was looking inside you.

Now she looked at him. She shifted her stance to one side and something crossed over her eyes. It was not a smile. But she saw him. The poem was short and by the time he stopped thinking about her hair, she was done.

She glanced at Mr. Wyeth.

"It was supposed to be a pantoum," she said and walked to her desk. "I'm not done with it."

Mr. Wyeth said it was fine like it was. He did not talk for a few seconds, and the students waited.

"Okay, Lise," he finally commanded.

Lise's tattoos were like henna on her arms. She held her hands in front of her, one hand resting in the other, and did not smile. She didn't need a paper because she knew her poem by heart.

She said, "In history we studied the supreme court. So that inspired this poem. See, in a hearing, a woman accused a wannabe judge of all but raping her. She was fifteen when it happened."

Lise paused to take a breath. Samir thought he should pause to take a breath, too, when his time came.

"'The Judge,'" she said.

She read a poem about a man who would become a judge, but in the poem a woman remembers when they were both teenagers. He assaulted her at a party and kept her quiet by nearly suffocating her with his hand.

A girl in the class cheered when Lise finished. Samir thought the judge would have had higher status than the girl. He knew how these things happened all the time. More, he thought Heera should move here as soon as possible and for the family to be together. They needed to have each other to talk to and learn how to live in this place.

Mr. Wyeth paused to discuss the tradition of political protest poems.

Samir heard his name called. He stood abruptly. In Nepal you stood when a teacher called your name. He took a breath.

He had prepared. He wore a white shirt loosely tucked into his jeans. His dark hair fell partly across his eyes.

He glanced at Olive. He had looked at Olive when he shoved her boyfriend at the cove. Maybe it happened when he was trying to get his balance. He hoped it gave him a certain standing with this girl.

Before he spoke, he began to draw at the whiteboard.

He drew quick long strokes on the board — the sway of an animal's back, the curve of the skull, the forelegs reaching forward, his tail as high as his mane.

He thought of the seven horses painting they were getting for the restaurant.

Hajurba had said, "The seven horses painting brings strength and success, and on horses you fly."

Samir began. Or rapped. He could pretend he was among the tall trees all alone. He stood wide-legged, and his heel tapped a slow beat.

> *You want to know my name?*
> *You can know like this.*
> *My homeland is Bhutan*
> *but I've never been there.*
> *I wait for them,*
> *all my brothers in Pathri.*
> *My brothers and sisters*
> *we dance in the field.*
> *On a horse we fly.*
> *You want to know my name?*
> *Wait is my name. I always wait for you,*
> *all my brothers in Pathri.*

He saw Olive's eyes that were bright, staring at the horse he drew.

"It's a portrait poem," Mr. Wyeth declared. "Where is Pathri?"

"My home in Nepal. I have a lot of memories of Pathri," Samir said.

But everybody was already standing to leave. It was the last day, the last class.

"Keep writing, Samir," Mr. Wyeth said, holding up his hand. "I'd like to read more."

Suddenly something caught Samir's eye in the open window beside the azaleas — a tall, loping guy got out of a red car in the parking lot. He knew.

Class was over. "Turn in your final poems," Mr. Wyeth called above the roar.

Samir had not moved. Gabe hung out by his car.

Samir wanted much more courage than he felt now. He couldn't fight with the son of Ethel's longtime customer. He couldn't lose his job, not when it gave him more value for his family.

He grabbed the strap of his pack and almost leapt into the air to get out of there. But people from the dance team were in the halls and pouring out the open door. They hugged Samir along with everybody else and shouted goodbye. More people from the dance team came to hug him. There was definitely more hugging here than in Worcester. There were girls from Puerto Rico and the Dominican Republic. They were good dancers and they got new moves off each other.

Coming down the steps and into the sidewalk, Olive passed by Samir and Lise who were talking. Olive never talked to him at school. But now she stopped and glanced at him like she was going to say something. It was not impossible. They did live across the street from each other.

But then they both heard Gabe shout from his car in the distance.

Olive looked over and whatever she might have said to

Samir, she didn't. He thought she didn't expect to see Gabe here. Her eyes opened with surprise as she said something to Lise. Then she ran to Gabe.

Students were packing up and heading to their cars or buses. Samir walked through the crowd. He had to cross by Gabe to get to the street. He couldn't *not* see Gabe. He was wearing a golf shirt or a polo shirt with a collar. Black. A company name Samir didn't take time to read was stitched over the pocket.

He didn't want to be this close to them, but he heard Olive say, "Good luck, your first day! Call me!" She hugged him.

Olive and Lise headed toward the back gym entrance where Lise's car was parked.

That left Gabe and Samir who froze a split second with their eyes on each other. Gabe's eyes were round and darkened like a street cat. He cocked his head. A taunt.

Samir turned. He hated himself for turning. He could have slammed the guy's eyes. He knew he couldn't because of his family. He was also shaking to imagine how fast Gabe could take him out.

13

OLIVE

"The boy," Olive's mother said. Olive had just come in from a job interview the day after school let out.

"What boy?"

Mom pointed across the street.

"The neighbor boy was carrying a bicycle."

Olive knew the rusted yellow bike the old man rode. Samir called him Hajurba. The bike was on the small side, a little bigger than a kid's bike.

"Somebody threw it in the creek," Mom said.

"What?" Olive said.

"I was walking after work and I saw the spokes in the creek. The bike was caught in a dead tree with the wheel spinning." Mom's eyes had circles underneath.

"That boy climbed in and got the bike loose and he

carried it." She opened her arms to show how he did it. "Carried it back to their house."

"How can they stand it here?" Olive said. "Did you see who threw it in the creek?"

Mom didn't answer. She smelled like paint and coffee. "That's a long way to carry a bike."

Olive's mind moved to the old man. She smiled when he pedaled.

"Who would do that?" she said.

She had talked to Gabe Wednesday night and she'd told him how she and Mom checked the window locks after hearing about the brick in the neighbor's window. She saw him for a second yesterday when he came by the school. In a manager's shirt with a collar! Maybe high school looked weird to him, seeing Olive in a stream of kids coming out the front doors. Last day. All the kids were wishing each other the best summer. Even the dance team had circled Samir. Gabe would have seen him in the team's huddle. She hadn't talked to Gabe since.

"Beats me," Mom said about who did it. "Now that's going to be all over the Creek Village Community Page."

In the kitchen, Olive and Mom leaned their hips into the counter and looked in the fridge. They couldn't face the leftover casserole.

Mom said, "Just remember, those people aren't our problem. Look at you. You should eat better. Don't eat like the jail girls. They don't eat healthy. Who could in that place?" She topped up her coffee, and they made grilled cheeses with tomato and slices of onion.

"I was glad to see Gabe got in at the bike shop."

Olive glanced at her. Could her mother know anything more?

She wanted her suspicions to be wrong. That Gabe was just reeling off his father's words. That Gabe just lost his temper sometimes.

"Yeah," she said. "Parts manager."

The sandwiches were good and crunchy. They rubbed their buttery fingers together.

And then Olive asked, "Did you see the boy?"

"I told you."

"I mean the one who stole it."

They looked at each other.

Mom said, "Leave it alone, will you? They've got nothing to do with us." Her phone rang and she left, the phone in one hand, half a sandwich in the other.

Olive went up to her room. It was a very green room.

A flash of a conversation hit her. She wanted that scrap of conversation, more than she wanted the festering worry about Gabe.

Chris had asked, "What would you call this green?"

"Grecian green," she'd said.

"Like green with a little milk."

"Yeah." She liked that. Green with a little milk in it.

In this green room, she took a breath. She called Gabe. He was working at the bike shop, his second day. He might not be able to answer.

Yesterday was big for them both. She was now a senior in high school. He was a manager at Powersports Plus.

He picked up.

"Can you talk?" she said.

"Just went on break."

He was worried, too. It was in his voice.

She wanted him.

He said, "I was freaked about starting this job, yesterday in the parking lot."

"You looked tense," she said.

"I didn't mean to take it out on you. What'd you do to your hair?"

"I cut it. What do you mean, take it out on me?"

"All the better to see your eyes."

What had he meant? Had he thrown the neighbor's bike in the creek? She just said it.

"Did you take it out on that family? You hate them."

She could tell he knew what she was talking about.

"It was Kyle," he said.

"What?"

"He had a couple bricks from the place where he's working."

"Kyle? You mean that morning at their window? Like a terrorist?"

"He had a brick. Not a bomb."

"You didn't tell me when I called you."

"I told you that you didn't have to be afraid. He likes those far-right sites. Some of it makes sense. There's 22 million illegal immigrants. The government opens the door to them. They give the Democrats power. This group Kyle's with calls for action. If we don't have a voice, we have to protest."

"Please stop talking," she said.

"It all makes sense."

"Stop," she said. "I want to talk about staying over with you."

He let a breath out.

Suddenly it felt too fast to go to Gabe's tomorrow. If she left, it would just be her mom in the house, checking the locks in the dark.

She said, "I'll come next weekend. I'm still looking for a job. I told Mom we'd both have jobs. I need to wait till then. Do you work Saturdays?"

"Till noon."

"I'll come then, next Saturday."

"Jesus, I'm glad," he said. That breath again.

They did not talk about any bicycle.

14

SAMIR

Bhim saw the bike in the creek first. He was pretending he had a fishing pole and could fish in the creek that was in the small woods behind the houses.

He saw Hajurba's bike and came yelling to Samir, who'd come home from work. They raced back through the playing field and down to the creek, and Samir kicked off his flip-flops and took his life in his hands to wade into the water. He almost panicked to feel the push of the tidal creek against his shins. It was like the water was alive and colder than snow. He did not want to learn to swim like his grandfather wanted. But he would get the yellow bike.

In the creek, he freed the spokes from the tree roots. The handlebars were mangled. Both tires were flat. Samir carried it home across the field, his arms around the frame like it was a wounded animal, while Bhim ran behind him.

At home, he leaned the bike beside the row of shoes that lined the living-room wall.

Hajurba wouldn't look. He went outside to dig up more garden dirt.

"I will fix it!" Samir called after him.

When Heera called, he wanted to talk about when they were children.

"Do you remember, Heera, when we were going to some relatives and we heard the bells from a temple? Ama told us how the mind holds the sound of the bell after it stops."

"Yes, of course," she said. "You okay?"

"I'm fine. I'm just remembering things. One day we were visiting the other uncles and we climbed a mountain and far away down below we could see the goats like small toys."

"Do you want to come back to Worcester?"

"No," he said. "I'm just remembering."

"You still have the bracelet I made last Bhai Tika?"

He dug in his pocket and pulled out a small knot of wooden beads and frayed red and yellow threads.

"Yeah," he said. "It stayed on the longest. It didn't fall off for a month."

"But you kept it."

He held up his palm to show her. She very seriously said she would make him another one this coming Bhai Tika.

She had on the big glasses that circled her eyes. She lifted her hands and twisted her hair to fall over her shoulder.

"Samir, it's funny what people say about Nepal. Even I have seen a poster here. It says if you want to wake up from life you have to go to visit Nepal." She laughed.

"I'm waiting for you. I can leave the café and we'll both work for Baba when you come."

"And we'll put that poster on the wall and all the people can tell us about their trip when they visited Nepal. And everyone will look at us and think that we are enlightened or something."

"Namaste," he said, teasing.

"Namaste. I'll see you tomorrow. You didn't forget we're coming for the weekend?"

"I didn't. Hurry up."

Samir took the bike to the porch. He released the tires, leaned the bike on the railing. When he pulled the inner tubes out, he found many leaks and began to patch the holes. Hajurba wiped mud off the frame. It was still good, but some of the spokes were broken, and Samir did not have the tools to fix them.

He called his father who was at work at Walmart. He didn't say where he found the bike, only that he didn't know how to replace spokes that were broken.

"Would you bring home a spoke tool kit with a spoke wrench? We need it for the bike."

At 11 p.m., the family's good friend Bishnu arrived at the door, a cigarette between his lips, a Nike cap pushed back over his bald spot, the carrom champion of Pathri. Behind him came Baba and Samir's uncle with more tools. They prepared food and opened beers. On the porch, they laid into the food. They ate, loud and laughing.

Bishnu told Samir in Nepali, "You want to learn to drive? I will take you. It won't be long and I will take you." He laughed. "I am a much better teacher than your father."

There was always teasing, but the men were also spread out across the porch and the lawn like security guards. They weren't going to talk about hooligans in front of Hajurba.

Then they all got to work on Hajurba's bike. They propped the old yellow bike upside down in the grass, with Hajurba watching. Uncle coached Samir to thread the spokes and replace the nipples. Not that it was easy, jockeying each other as they did and stopping to eat and drink and tell jokes, so it took a few hours.

That's how it happened that Hajurba, in his cap and white trousers, pedaled his bike around the yard under the moon at 2 a.m. But he was very sad. He treated the bike like an injured animal that he loved and could not protect.

The next day on the first Saturday of summer vacation, Bhim raced down the street on the same yellow bike. He met Samir at the corner when he got a short break from the café. It was almost ten. Any minute, Heera and Ama would come.

"Let's race," Bhim called out.

"You're too fast. I can't beat you." Samir's flip-flops slapped on the concrete.

Bhim looped around him twice and then set off alone to his house, calling, "Ama, Ama! It's time to cook for Dai."

When Samir got to his gate, he saw Bhim riding past Olive on her porch swing. He was doing tricks and showing off for her. He showed her how he could ride fast and how he could ride with no hands. The traffic was constant with drivers using their street to reach downtown.

Olive called to him, "You're not that big, and any car

speeding up the road might not see you."

"I am big!" Bhim sang, standing on his toes on the pedals.

Olive called again. "You want to decorate your bike?"

Samir knew this would sound good to Bhim. He liked to make friends. He made friends with the lady at the Day Night. He chatted with people on the sidewalk. He made friends with every person in the church thrift store.

Olive left and returned with a box of bright-colored items. Bhim was by her side, stretching and popping them. They were something like the cloth-covered hair elastics Heera wore, but Olive would no longer be able to use because she had cut her nice hair. Then she brought out reams of ribbons.

"Pick a ribbon," she said.

Samir paused at his fence. He could hear them. She showed Bhim how to make a piece of ribbon as long as his outstretched arms. Then they folded the ribbon in half. It was like watching them dance with their arms. They tied ribbons to the elastics. They raced to the street, and this girl showed Bhim how to stretch the elastics over the bike's handlebars, and the wind made the ribbon tails swirl.

"Colors," he called to Samir.

"Very nice," Samir said, but not loud. He tried not to look at Olive and suspected she knew the person who had tried to destroy Hajurba's bike.

"It's time to go, Bhim," he said from the gate.

"Your name is Bhim?" she asked.

He nodded. "What is yours?"

"Olive."

"That's a tree!"

"Yeah, I'm a tree." She lifted her arms and they both laughed.

Bhim wanted to make more streamers with Olive. He slid an elastic with streamers around Olive's wrist. She slid one around his upper arm, and then she glanced at Samir. She wore shorts and it looked like a bathing suit top that tied at the back of her neck. Her lips were pressed. He could tell she wished him gone.

Bhim pedaled off with multicolored streamers flowing from his bike.

"No one could miss seeing you now," Olive sang out. The streamers blew high as he pedaled.

"Ama, Ama," he screamed to his mother. She came out, passing by Samir as he climbed up the porch steps. "Look at all my colors," Bhim called.

"We should go in," Samir called after them. Baba had said he should watch Auntie and Bhim and Hajurba.

"Yes," Bhim's ama said. But she brought out marigolds made of sheer cloth that were bright yellow, and they tied the marigolds on the streamers, too. The streamers grew more beautiful.

Samir wished he could be there when the cars began to arrive. But he would not risk anything with Ethel. Also, Samir working in a café would show his importance to the family. He'd have to wait until after work to see the family he missed.

All of Samir's family was here in his house. Ama, Heera, Baba, Hajurba, Auntie and Uncle and Bhim, Baba's school-hood friend, his wife and two children.

The house and the outside seemed to expand for them.

He heard his mother talking very fast as she always did. Her voice carried from the backyard — sometimes low, sometimes loud and laughing. He ran up the porch stairs into the kitchen, where more people were chopping and sautéing and stirring. He opened the back door to the small area where Auntie fed the birds.

But now his parents stood in a triangle of sunlight, heaving rocks from the soil past the trees that were now farther back than they were before Ama came just a few hours ago. They had cut down spindly trees and shrubs and turned over new earth.

"What is this?" Samir said.

"We have made room for the sun," Baba said. They spoke in Nepali.

Ama wore the small black boots she always wore, tight jeans and a baggy shirt. She rested the handle of the hoe against her ribs, then she opened and closed her fingers like stars to relieve her muscles. At the same time, she looked at Samir, and he watched her smile spread across her entire face and into her eyes.

She said, "Hello, baby," and he didn't mind like he usually did. She opened her arms wide. He hugged her.

"We are expanding the garden."

Together she and Baba named all the things they would plant when Heera and Ama moved to Mersea by the end of the summer.

"Spinach, potato, Dalle peppers, eggplant, cabbage, cauliflower, radish, bitter gourd." Ama and Baba looked at each other and laughed.

"You were born a farmer's son," Baba announced.

"I know," Samir said. "You told me."

"And now you are the son of a farmer who owns a restaurant." Ama glowed.

That's why everyone was here. This was the celebration party weekend. His parents were so happy. Baba had also installed a floodlight above the door for security.

Now Baba would turn on this brightness and check in the night to see who might be in the open space where the trees used to be.

Ama put her arm around Samir's waist and walked him into the kitchen.

She set to work with the other cooks. She turned the jasmine rice upside down on a platter. They had made dahi chiura, kwati, the soup made with nine beans, roti, long noodles for good luck and prosperity, purple grapes for the wealth of the restaurant and — specially for Samir — chow mein, his favorite dish. He liked the crispy noodles with chicken or shrimp or without.

Ama, Auntie and Uncle served up plates of food for each person. Samir and Heera helped the little children carry their plates. The kitchen was hot with the heat of the night and cooking. They sat on the red wooden chairs, some on the porch steps, some sat cross-legged in the warm grass of the lawn or on a mat.

Heera and Samir sat with Bhim and Bishnu's kids. Hajurba wore his jacket and cap.

Ama had gone to change her clothes for the party. Now with Ama in the house, Hindi pop music played loudly in the background. Then she appeared in a sari draped around her shoulder. She had outlined her eyes in black and brushed her eyelids in blue and over the blue, a sky of glitter. She was dressed for a celebration with a lot of jewelry. Many photos were taken of Baba and Ama. Then Baba, Ama, Heera and Samir. Pictures were taken of Ama and her secret momos. Photos were taken of Samir who was grinning with a full plate of chow mein. Movies were made of all the people, the plates of food, and some people swayed to the sound of the tabla and bansuri.

With these photographs, the Paudels would talk to the family back in the camps and in Bhutan. They would show, Look, we are thriving. We are the renters of a space to open a restaurant. We have a loan. We are business people in America.

There were many photos of Samir and Heera, because every success was for them, the children.

Heera had made milk tea with pepper root and cardamom for Hajurba. He sipped it from his cup that he liked — the one with the state bird of New Hampshire.

It was then that Bishnu spoke up. He had heard good things about Nebraska from their cousins who lived there. He began to describe their cousins' house. Maybe they could get a better house for less money in Nebraska.

Samir and Heera exchanged glances. They had heard these words many times before. One elder would get an idea to move to a new place where they would have a better life. Baba and Bishnu as teenaged boys had moved from place to place trying to make enough money to survive. In America, sometimes people kept on moving.

Uncle said, "How much are the rents in Nebraska?" On his phone, he began to check.

Samir waited for Baba to answer him, to tell him that soon they could afford to buy this house and when they did, they would build on. They would make it a two-story house with three bedrooms or four.

But Baba leaned back in his Real Madrid soccer shirt, put his hands on his hips and listened.

Auntie said, "We have a big space for a garden here." She held up her small hands to show she had the dirt of New Hampshire under her fingernails.

"A garden!" Bishnu shouted. "We can make farms wherever we go."

He began to sing the nostalgic song of friendship when farmers called out to each other as they plowed behind their oxen. Samir had played this song many times for Hajurba on YouTube — *Hariyo dada mathi halo jotne saathi* — and Hajurba tried to teach Samir the words. But Samir was learning higher level math with Mr. Parrish who was also the dance team advisor and was not interested in practicing Nepali.

Everyone was talking.

"How far away is Nebraska?" Heera called out to Samir.

"I'm not going to Nebraska," Samir said.

She turned her head curiously to him. He did not respond to her. The day Samir was late to the gym because he was stacking the peaches for Ethel at the café, he had told Mr. Parrish he was sorry.

Mr. Parrish said, "Practice is over. You missed the practice."

Samir felt shame and said, "I'm sorry. I will leave the dance team."

"Samir, you *are* the dance team. Just don't be late next time."

Samir hated what Gabe was doing — evidence or not, Samir knew it was Gabe — and he knew he couldn't tolerate it. Not one more thing. He also knew he wanted to be on the Mersea High dance team. He wanted to stay for his senior year.

He stood up in his backyard with all the people talking loudly. He had never spoken the way he was about to. He had always deferred to what his family needed. What his family needed, he needed also. He thought his father had a dream and it was here. Samir had to tell his father his position.

"Baba, I am not moving." That was it. "I am not moving." He said, "What if I have friends here?"

He did not. Samir's wish was that some kid would text him and say, Hey, do you want to hang out? Maybe he was as homesick for friends from Pathri as Hajurba was. Maybe not. Sometimes people slapped Samir on the back after a performance. They wanted him to teach Bollywood dance to the middle-school kids.

"I am not moving again. I am staying here. I will help you with the restaurant."

Heera stood beside him, her glasses sparkling, and a half-moon appeared high in the sky and the torch light softly lit the corner of the porch.

"Me, too, Baba. I will be really good with the customers. *Please come. We are honored you will be part of our delicacy. You are about to experience the taste of Nepal.*"

Ama put her arms around each of her children who were already taller than she was.

"Right here we have a taste of Nepal. Eat, eat."

Baba brought his son a new plate of chow mein.

"You have hardly eaten," he said.

That's what Baba did. If Samir was focused on homework and fell asleep without eating, Baba would come to wake him up with a plate of curry or choila or maam and insist that Samir sit up right now and eat.

Hajurba listened to Bishnu talk on about the places they could go and put down their roots. Samir could imagine Hajurba with his duffle carrying his essential things — their aluminum pot, the gundruk, tea, the rum pum, his items of clothing, his school books with the pictures he drew for his teacher, his mouthwash, the comb.

And the yellow bicycle.

15

OLIVE

Mom was supposed to be home from work. There was a special program this afternoon with the women's kids that had kept her late, but this was past late.

A little while later, Olive's phone rang.

"My car's broken down," Mom said. "I'm still at the jail. I've called Julia but there's no answer. Could you find Gabe and see if he'll give me a ride? Is he with you?"

"He's supposed to be here any minute. I'll come with him."

Olive waited on the porch. The heat pressed on her skin.

Gabe pulled up in front of the house. He took a second to stand in the street while he stared over at Samir's house and all the people.

She ran to his car and got in the driver's seat. Gabe was beside her in a heartbeat. Gabe and Chris had always let her drive.

Pulling off Chestnut Street was a huge relief. Just her and Gabe. She glanced at him.

"I miss you," she whispered.

She wanted to tell him about Bhim. Tell him that he was a regular kid and they made bike streamers together. She wanted Gabe to meet him. He was such a funny kid.

But when she looked at Gabe, she realized if she told him about Bhim, he might start in again about immigrants.

Her phone rang again. "We're on our way, Mom."

Olive drove the rattly Prius. They didn't talk, but she felt the warmth of his hand on her leg and she was melting.

At the jail, Olive jumped out of the car. But Gabe climbed over the gear to the driver's seat and grabbed her hand through the window. She stopped still, rested herself on Gabe's neck, in his smell. She looked toward the door, feeling like she was naked in the parking lot under the drooping American flag and the spotlights.

Olive heaved open the front door that led to a lobby where a guard sat behind a glass window. The waiting room had coloring books and wooden puzzles for little children coming to see their family here.

Mom came out looking really tired and got in the car beside Gabe. She straightened her back and turned her exhausted eyes to take them in.

"Thanks," she said to Gabe.

"Not a problem," he said.

It was just so natural that now they were all a family.

"The clutch. Or the alternator," Mom said. "Chris always fixed it."

"Don't mind taking a look," Gabe said.

On the hot June night, the Prius rocked and bumped its dented red body up the New Hampshire highway.

At home, Gabe said he'd borrow his dad's truck and tow Mom's car up to his place, where he had tools and a three-sided shed.

"Back to the college applications," he said. "If they give me a break, maybe I'll get some grant money out of this. Probably not. There's strings to get shit."

Mom went inside the screen door.

"Aren't you coming in?" Olive said to him.

"Why don't you come out to our house like we planned? They're dead asleep. We got the whole place. Then I'll bring you home."

She wanted him right now, this whole night she had. What if that fixed everything?

The music was loud across the street.

"Holy crap," he said. "How can you stand it? We're getting out of here." He took her hand. Even his hand felt like sex.

And then her words spat out. "We decorated the bike."

"What bike?"

"Their bike. The little boy and I. We decorated the handlebars with about a hundred scrunchies. And the ribbons we tied on the scrunchies were every color and they flapped in the wind so people could see him. On the bike they dragged out of the creek."

She didn't let go of his hand.

She said, "I love you. So does my mom. Leave them alone."

He shook his head. "You just don't get it, do you?"

She shrugged. He held her hand tighter.

"Come to my car," he said.

"I'm only human." She was actually laughing.

They raced to the street and his car. It was parked in the dark. He swung the back door open.

It stank like always.

They fit in the back seat fine. On top of each other.

No talking.

The car rocked, neither of them cared a hoot.

When he left, the Prius puffed out little farts as it descended the hill. It wasn't supposed to do that. She hoped it wasn't toast.

She sang from the porch steps. "I'm never gonna let you go."

She turned and saw a sprig of something green in a plastic seed pot no bigger than a porcelain creamer sitting to the side of the doorsill.

Olive took it to Mom in the kitchen. Mom felt the tiny prickles on the stem.

"It's a little rose," Olive said. "Who would give us a rose?"

"Somebody who knows how to start a rose from seed," Mom said. "It takes a long time. You have to collect the rose hips, like the lady across the street. She showed me."

"She showed you?" Olive asked.

"I asked what all those pots were on her porch."

Olive went in the art room with the big picture window. Their yard wasn't that big, but they used to have a vegetable garden and grapes that trailed on the fence, and a thorny rose Chris called the briar patch.

"Mom," Olive said. "Let's make a garden."

"Why?"

"We have a rose." It only had five leaves, but it was a rose.

Mom looked at the rose. They looked out the window at the stalks and weeds.

Mom straightened up. "We don't have a car. But we can have a garden."

They put on wellies and walked in the wet soil.

They hauled out branches and leaves, crumbling bricks from a path grown over. They found the old rose bush still alive and gave it some space. They bound bundles of sticks and branches with twine.

They kept working until there was an outline of the moon in the sky.

Then they cooked burgers that they ate on bright-colored plates sitting out on a bench so rickety they swayed on it.

"Eat fast, before the bench collapses," Mom said.

Olive was streaked with mud. Then they planted the rose on the edge of the garden. It looked okay there in the moonlight.

"What about the ashes?" Mom said.

"Do you mean like here?"

"At least talk about what Chris would've wanted."

"He'd be glad to see us working our asses off," Olive said. "Making a rose grow."

"Hope nothing happens to Gabe," Mom said. "Sometimes he gets in his own damn way."

"What do you mean?"

"He and Chris were good for each other. I mean, Gabe's father's a mean bastard. But Chris was a kind of check on all that meanness."

"But you still like him."

"I'd give him the moon," she said. "But how do you tell a kid to stay clear of his dad?"

16

SAMIR

Samir was FaceTiming Heera.

"Your visit was too short," he said. "If you were still here, I would be happy."

"You've changed."

"Because I said I wasn't moving?"

"No, you've always been stubborn. But before you used to be a little bit fun. You were always upside down with your feet in the air. You were always dancing even when you played Machha Machha Bhyaguta with Bhim."

"I'm fun. I still like Fishy Fishy Frog." Samir was trying to tease the solemn look from Heera's eyes.

"What about that boy, Gabe? Is he still your neighbor's boyfriend?"

Samir's eyes snapped back to her. He didn't want there

111

to be any connection between his sister and Gabe. He was angry that she knew his name.

"I guess," he said.

"Who is he?"

"No one you want to know," Samir said.

"I could explain to him. Like how cool you are."

Samir shook his head. "No," he said, walking away from the phone. "There's no explaining. There is only letting people like him out of our minds. Don't talk about him."

"Is he why you're changing?"

"Look," Samir said softly. He wanted to bring them to a good place.

Just a day ago Heera had been here in the kitchen telling him and Auntie stories of Worcester.

"What's Olive doing? Bhim said he teased her for being named for a tree."

"Heera, you know the people here better than I do."

"You said her name — Olive, our neighbor."

Our neighbor. They were already a family here.

"Why didn't you introduce me to her? I want a haircut like hers. Samir, you should invite her over and make her some kheer."

"No!" he said. "And don't cut your hair!"

"Now you're acting old-fashioned."

"I would never invite her over," Samir clarified. "But Bhim talks about her like she's our sister. If she came, it would be normal. I could be normal."

"You are not normal. You dance like Tiger Shroff. Try looking at a girl the way Tiger looks at a girl, Dai." Heera laughed. "You know, like he lifts his chin with a little smirk.

Yeah, you should practice looking at girls that way."

They both had to go, and when her face disappeared, he missed even the interrogation.

In the morning he got up at five to prepare for work. Hajurba sat cross-legged at the shrine. Ama had placed a new tulsi plant beside it. Samir smelled its scent of a peppery spice and he knew Ama was getting ready to cook here all the time. She would drop leaves from the plant into her stews.

He nearly tripped over the yellow bike in the front doorway. Every night they brought the bike in the house, like Hajurba said they had to bring the bikes inside at the refugee camp so villagers didn't steal them. In the back, the spotlight shone on the young garden plants to protect their house from vandalizers.

Was this how to live in America? He knew Baba was researching more security systems. Samir, though, woke up with a long, burning worry about Gabe.

He tried to control the thoughts in his mind with the scent of Ama's tulsi plant. He tried to turn his mind to learning every day about American restaurants at his job, even though he spent many hours vigilant about who would come through the café door. Samir was determined to listen and record in his mind what happened in the business.

In his imagination, he'd be Tiger Shroff and sometimes leap onto the counter between the coffee mugs and belt out a song of pure joy that he had got himself a job in New Hampshire and it was warm and summer. He could walk home and bring a paycheck and Baba would be proud.

Samir walked down the city street and along the path from the parking lot and up the stairs to the River's Tale door.

The wind gusted and flipped the birch leaves facing up and down. He tried on the idea that the people at the River's Tale were loyal to each other the way his father was loyal to Bishnu and his other friends who had been deported with him. Samir was envious that the people at the River's Tale could see each other every day, but his father's friends and his friends were scattered across the world.

And now in this place, hadn't his parents transformed their dark backyard into the open space in the sunlight when they cleared and dug and hoed a forest into the family's garden?

17

OLIVE

Olive had an interview for the day-camp counselor job she'd spotted. She needed to work and get away from the neighbors.

She stood in the shower and let the water wash through her hair. It took out the white paint wax and the orange fringe. She was back to her regular color, but it was still cropped.

She let it dry in the sun and it got wavy. She wore striped socks and lace-up boots and her favorite thin sweater.

She did her ride through the Creek Village neighborhood, then the route to the north side of Mersea. Her mind went to Chris and how he knew the land and the water. He thought the sea had a memory and would come back at high tide like somebody coming home.

Then he was there, loping beside her.

Hey, he said.

Ohhh.

She slowed down. She could not say no. Just one more time. Next time she'd tell him she had to go.

She sucked in her breath. He smelled like chocolate. Damn, he even had chocolate on his hands.

It melted, he complained.

Well, that sucks. Oh, God, could she make it last June again? And after the interview, they'd get pancakes at the River's Tale.

I remember that sweater, he said. *It's so flimsy, when you ride, it looks like a butterfly's wings.*

He smiled at her like she was born to fly, and she couldn't even decide how to make it through the summer, when all she wanted was for things to be the way they were, with Gabe and Chris and her, wild kids.

Fishing tonight.

He was gone. She had to catch her breath. She always had to do that when he came, and she had to let him go. It had been like that the last year of his life. So much crying when Olive and Mom couldn't get him into treatment because, they said, he still had a job. *Your brother can go a week without using. There are folks who can't go a day.*

She turned into the gate of the North Mersea Rec Center. She left her bike at the back of the building beside the big tires for kids to swing in, a long slide and a jungle gym. In the woods, campers and counselors had built a campground. They had a sink with a hose and a countertop of small tree trunks, lots of stick houses a child could squat-walk inside, a whole pretend home outdoors in the woods.

Her interview was with the education director for this

neighborhood summer camp, Mr. Farley. He was about Olive's height, built like a block with bright eyes.

"You sent in your Basic Swimming Instructor certificate?" he began.

"Yes, and I've been swimming since I was two."

He explained that they didn't intentionally swim in the creek, but sometimes kids fell in.

"So, lifesaving," she said.

He laughed. "Not usually. We're an environmental-education operation. Counselors guide the kids into the forest to explore the habitat. Nature crafts. Singing. Safety. Always safety first."

"I can show them how to make fishing poles out of a fallen apple branch."

"These kids would like to turn apple branches into fishing poles. There's a lot of magic in the woods. Why do you want to work here, Olive?"

This was a place where no one was doing drugs or was sad about people doing drugs. It could be a place just for Olive without Gabe or her mom.

"I like kids," Olive finally offered. The only young kid she currently knew was Bhim. Simone was growing up. "And I know about nature. We grew up not far from the creek."

"And you have a lifesaving certificate. Let's set you up for a counselor slot. It's $17 per hour."

Mr. Farley said he'd send the papers for her to fill out. She needed to bring them back and a copy of her birth certificate — to prove she wasn't a foreign alien, she guessed.

She decided not to go home. It was summer. Gabe was at work. Mom was at work.

Olive turned south to the lift bridge over the river. From the camp, it was a half-hour ride to see Lord of the Fishes. For good luck.

She rode through the downtown, then through the cemetery. She hadn't been to the cove since that night with Gabe. It crossed her mind that trouble was in this place, but it drew her.

She rode down the rocky path to the spur of land and the beach. Across was the small island.

Sure enough, the spotted horse was still there beside the abandoned house with the long windows and gables. She saw a man come across the bridge to take the horse into the lean-to, and maybe the horse got some oats.

How could there be anything so sad as one horse?

There was something about this place. So abandoned. So serene because the waves were more gentle in the cove. And desolate with fallen trees and not a sea rose in sight.

18

SAMIR

The horse whistled. Samir froze.

He had just come to the cove. He was at the place where the trees still grew.

Then he saw the girl. She stood at the edge of the water. He instantly turned to look for Gabe. He listened for footsteps in the woods or the snap of a stick on the path.

Olive began to take off her sweater. Was she going to swim?

Samir backed away. He did not want to embarrass her by watching her undress.

But she didn't. She took off her boots and kept on her shorts and top. The air was warm. He watched her splash into the cold water and imagined the small, cold stones under her feet that he'd seen when the tide pulled out.

The horse whinnied again. She waded out. He felt amazement at her courage, and shame that he was afraid of the water. She dived into the sparkling river as if she had the momentum to swim across to the island. She even nose-dived underwater and flew sideways along the current. Then she made long strokes with her arms through the water.

He imagined what it would feel like to pull his own arms through the water. And make the water blur as he kicked his feet.

Then she rolled to her back. The sun would cause her to shut her eyes.

Samir lifted his gaze to the sun. His eyes shut and the world looked on fire with purple and orange.

Then his eyes sprang open and he spun around. Where was Gabe?

Samir began to believe that she was alone. He was trying to think of a way that he could signal his presence so that it didn't seem like he was sneaking up on her.

He tried to imitate the whinny of the horse but it came out much louder than he meant. It pierced through the air over the water, and the girl leapt like a fish half out. She spun around to face the shore.

She saw him. He had stepped onto the sand and stood very still with his feet apart. He whistled again to tell her, Yes, I happen to be here. This is an accident that I'm here the same time as you.

The horse whinnied in return. She looked around. She would see he was alone. She'd see the yellow bike with streamers leaning against a birch tree.

"This is my beach. Did you follow me?" Olive yelled.

"Why would I follow you?" he called.

Olive ran out of the water shivering.

"This is also my beach," he said.

She pulled on her holey sweater and grabbed her boots.

"I thought that bike was busted. Someone threw it in the creek," she said.

They stood there for a few seconds. He had come because he was trying to build his courage to go in the water. The girl was graceful and strong in the water.

All he knew was that just for this second, he didn't want her to go.

"You come for the horse?" he said.

"I come for my brother," she said.

"Did he go away?"

"Yes."

Samir didn't understand. But he could tell she didn't want to say any more.

He said, "My grandfather lost someone in the river. In Nepal. The river was very, very fast."

She waited.

"He likes to come and sing to this person."

"Here?"

"Yes. His English teacher brought his class here for a picnic and she told them that used to be a school." Samir pointed to the building on the island. "My grandfather sings wherever he is. He sings for happiness, he sings for sadness, he sings when someone dies."

Then he got an idea. It was a spontaneous idea and probably stupid.

"Can I ask a favor?"

"I don't even know you."

He ignored that. She knew him.

"Now that school is out, my job lasts later at River's Tale Café. But I need to walk my grandfather and aunt to their English class. Their last day of school is tomorrow."

"Why can't they walk themselves?"

"It's not safe."

She studied him, suspicious. "What could happen?"

"Someone needs to walk with them," he said. "My father if not me. They are afraid because of the bike. And other things."

"I can't." She took off barefoot up the path where she left her bike.

"Their class starts at ten," he called. "My aunt likes you because you helped her son. You decorated the bike."

"It was just so drivers can see him!"

"He calls you sister," Samir said.

She began to run.

"Someone broke our window. They were throwing bricks."

She turned. He pushed the rubber wristbands he wore up his arms and waited. He remembered how she had watched him when he sang in Mr. Wyeth's class. And he could tell she liked the horse he drew on the board.

"I know," she called. "They should pay for it."

"My father told my aunt to stay inside. He called the police but they are still looking for who did it."

There was a jump in her eyes and he thought, *She knows.*

"I don't want to put you in a hard position," he said.

So why was he? He knew she was Gabe's girlfriend. But

of the white girls he'd met, he wanted to talk to this one. Like somehow they already knew each other.

Olive stood with her feet in the moss. Shadows of leaves danced in her hair which was too short, he thought, but it could grow back.

There was something between them. Samir could not know what. But he had asked her for something he had never asked of someone outside his own family.

He imagined her sitting across from Gabe at a booth at the River's Tale and she tells him, *Samir asked me to do a favor.* And they would laugh. Or she would not tell him. And she would not laugh.

Again, he did not want to cause problems for her. He wondered about her. Where was her brother?

"Come to the River's Tale." Their eyes met. He moved toward the shore. "I'll walk them that far. You can walk the rest of the way to the high school. It's their last class." He repeated the time.

He meant keep it a secret. From Gabe. It was a risk at the River's Tale, but Samir had not seen Gabe since the day with the peaches.

Was this a payoff for a debt? They never mentioned what Gabe did the last time they were here at the cove. But it felt more like she was just the girl across the street and in his English class and that's how they knew each other.

Heera said, *Make room for one American friend.*

"Why'd you draw that horse in Mr. Wyeth's class?" Olive was almost up to the path.

"To my grandfather," he called, "it is about traveling far in your mind. Like from one life to another. He has many superstitions. It is about flying. On the horse a person can fly."

He could feel her studying him like she had no idea what to make of him. But he was not invisible. And then she sped away on her own bike.

19

OLIVE

Olive imagined telling Gabe that Samir had asked her for a favor. That would put a fire in him.

She could hear his voice. "Remember what they told your mom in the jail training? You can't bring the inmates anything. They're always testing you. You take 'em a Tootsie Roll and they know they got you. They know down the road you'll bring them whatever they ask."

The next morning at quarter to ten, Olive went to the River's Tale in the building like a shack down from the strip mall where there was also the post office, a hair salon and what had been a mom-and-pop but it turned into a CVS like everything did, Lise said, thanks to corporate greed.

Olive was not going to tell Gabe. Was that fear? Of course not. He'd get riled. It was just walking to the school.

Olive also remembered the little boy laughing so loud that he spit when they made streamers and she felt like a kid herself for a little bit. Maybe Bhim would come and they'd laugh.

Samir was by the small back deck of the River's Tale. With him was his grandfather in a hat with zigzag designs around it and the lady in a sari with a Market Basket plastic bag over something in her arms. Bhim bopped around.

Samir was annoyed like he'd been with the lawn mower, but when Olive didn't go away, he must have realized she'd come to walk his family to the school. He looked like he didn't want to let her.

Bhim took her hand and Olive didn't leave.

Auntie said to Olive, "Hello my name Geeta." She lifted her hands to touch. Olive waved.

Samir's face gradually softened — not to a smile, but less frozen. She knew he hadn't counted on her, and Olive hadn't counted on herself, but she came.

He nodded.

She scrunched up her face. She wore a ball cap with the bill pulled low.

He said, "This is my grandfather, Mahendra Paudel. This is my aunt."

Mr. Paudel held the handlebars of the bicycle with the streamers. The bike was buffed and shiny.

He was telling her something, and Ms. Geeta said, "He want to tell you that the bright yellow of his bike reminds him of Dashain — our festival."

Olive could have told her, *My mother likes the rose*, but she didn't.

"Hajurba wipes down the bike every morning," Samir said, not looking at her.

"Sentimental." Ms. Geeta pronounced each syllable. "You think bike is like donkey."

Bhim spun the streamers around his arms. They stayed bunched up and headed out.

Samir waited at the café door. He would get in trouble with Ethel, Olive thought. Ethel was a tough boss.

They made it to the intersection — the grandfather on the bike, Bhim dancing, the aunt in the lead. Olive didn't know what to call the aunt so she decided to call her Ms. Geeta.

"Bhaanji!" Mr. Paudel called to Ms. Geeta — something that sounded like a command. They crossed to a sidewalk. Then Ms. Geeta shouted back at Mr. Paudel. At a crosswalk they forded the street with traffic coming and going quickly around them.

Bhim kept hold of Olive's hand. He danced her several blocks to the school. Ms. Geeta led them to a classroom and a teacher who looked like an early suffragette with flowy sleeves and wispy hair piled on her head. She might have been their kindergarten teacher — the one Chris said had a kind face, a funny kind because that cracked him up, a way he loved to tease Olive.

"Hi, Mahendra. Hi, Geeta," the teacher sang.

Mr. Paudel called, "Good morning, Daughter," to his teacher.

"Neighbor," Ms. Geeta said to introduce Olive.

"You brought Olive Ronan for the party. I remember you," their teacher said. "Welcome."

"I'm not staying," Olive said. She crossed her arms across her stomach and didn't budge from the door. But she was curious. The tiny classroom was a jungle of plants. On the walls were drawings of temples and black-spotted cows and tiny houses on green arrows that she could tell stood for hills. Bhim told her where to sit, beside him.

Another student arrived. Tia had dark curly hair and wheeled in a stroller with a kid who also had a headful of loose curls — a tiny replica of herself.

"She is Brazil," Ms. Geeta said and pointed out the enormous country of Brazil on a wall map of the world almost as big as the room.

"Show where you are from," the teacher said. Ms. Geeta showed a dot surrounded by Tibet and India.

Tia laughed at the largeness of Brazil and the dot of Bhutan, which made Olive step up to the map.

"You're from the Himalayas?" She hadn't known exactly where the Himalayas were until she saw the mountains looming on the map.

"When sun sets in Bhutan," Ms. Geeta said, "we see the foothills of the mountains." She pulled out her plate of food from its wrap, and a sweet smell wafted across the room. "Nepali donut," she said.

Tia added an enormous tray of what looked like tamales. More students came with their children and each added food to the table.

"Open your notebooks," the teacher said.

Hajurba was focused on her.

"For our last day, draw a window," the teacher said. She walked to a window in the classroom and opened it.

"Window," she said. "I opened the window."

"Yes," Mr. Paudel said.

"Draw your window." She pointed at him, then touched her head. "Like you remember."

"Yes." Mr. Paudel was waiting like they had done this many times to begin a class. The teacher passed out colored pencils.

Olive stood and waved to Bhim, *I'm going*. But he got a piece of drawing paper for her and gave her pencils.

"Window," he said.

She could think of windows. Windows she and Gabe had fogged up in his car. The picture window in the art room. She and Chris had finger painted horses on the glass. Even thinking of it made her smell the finger paint.

Olive sat for a second with Bhim and drew the picture window using the green marker. The windowsill, the flowers, the berries all were green. Green with a little milk in it. She painted with her brother.

And then the rain started to flow outside the classroom window. It beat on the window glass.

She gave a tiny signal to Bhim to say she had to go, then headed out the classroom door. The door led to an outside courtyard. She slid down the concrete wall and let the rain beat down around her. Her brother became the wall and they sat back-to-back.

With her narrow back pressed up against her brother's, she felt how much she could not bear this June. Being with Gabe was the natural, good thing. They already had a plan. They had each other. They would always have each other.

With Gabe this summer, she would put it back together.

Bhim came out in the rain and took cover with Olive. She let herself look at his snub nose.

"Get out of the rain. Go."

But he came closer and squatted down. He brought her the picture she drew, in a roll. Then he gave her a second rolled-up paper.

"Hajurba said to give this to you." Then he gave her a Nepali donut.

She sighed. She tucked the donut in her pocket.

Together they unrolled the second picture. Olive kept her elbows hugged in to keep the paper close and out of the rain as she opened it.

It looked like a picture of the derelict house on the little island.

Hajurba had drawn the tall windows of that house. In front he drew a stick-figure boy in trousers and cap. Beside it he wrote *School* on the paper.

He also drew a stick horse with four stick legs, a mane, a flying tail, a line for a head. Beside it was *Horse.*

20

SAMIR

Samir and his father took the *For Lease* sign down from the window of the building on the busy commercial street of Mersea. The Paudels' future restaurant.

Baba's gaze held his son hard and steady, his eyes narrowed with worry.

"I have given you a lot of responsibility, Samir. Maybe too much. But this is ours now. You see the restaurant, yes?"

"Yes, Baba."

His father was stern. Samir tried to think of him as a boy his age before the young men and students were arrested and taken from their farms. Or fled, like his father.

In front of Baba and Samir was an ordinary low brick building. Their restaurant was beside an eyelash business with a sign — *Lash Extensions, Brow Shaping, Bridal Makeup.*

On the far side of the eyelash business was a Chinese take-out. Bishnu, who ran his own grocery shop, advised them they should open a restaurant near a busy Chinese takeout. Good business.

"Now you know why so much is at stake. Yes?"

"I know," Samir said.

Baba was going to talk about fighting.

When Baba was very assertive, his voice grew softer and more serious.

"You need to take all AP classes. Yes. Are you doing that?"

"I'll be taking AP," Samir said.

"You have done well in your studies," Baba said. He switched to English. "I am proud. But you cannot stop."

"I will not stop, Baba."

"This is good. Don't let up," he said. "Use your summer to prepare for these classes. Do you have worries? Your mother heard from Heera that you are homesick."

"I'm okay. I want us to be together."

"We are working hard to do this."

"I know. Are you worried, Baba?"

Baba and Samir didn't often open up about feelings, so this was a strange question for both of them.

Baba hesitated. Then he said, "All is well."

In Pathri they told stories about America. Everyone in America had a goal. In America, they worked all the time.

Here's what Samir knew about Bhutan, where he had never been. All his family lived close together on a mountainside. There were three houses — first uncle, second uncle, first aunt. Farther on was their grandparents' big house where the other relatives lived together. Even relatives who were very distant stayed in the grandparents' house a long time, maybe a few years, until they could build their own house on the mountain. If a son was married but was not ready to build his own house, he and his whole family stayed in Hajurba and Hajurama's house until they had the money to build.

Boys went to school. Girls went a little while. The girls worked at home, keeping the cows and goats. Ama said she had a school dress and a home dress. She had one pair of flip-flops. She said you take off your shoes while walking to school to save them. At school you put on your shoes and stand in line. The teacher inspects your nails, rubs your skin and beats you with a cane if there is any dirt.

In the camp, they had two pairs of flip-flops.

Baba's homeland was Bhutan. Samir wasn't sure about his own. Was his homeland Nepal since he was born in the camp? But Nepal didn't want the Bhutanese Nepali. He had no country, Bhutan or Nepal.

After twenty years in the refugee camp, Hajurba was afraid to go to America. He wanted to return to his farm. But he was old, and his fear was not as great as his hope for Samir and Heera.

Everything now depended on Samir, first born.

Samir was aware of his father's steady, drumbeat walk. His father knew about violence. Some Lhotshampas — southern people like Samir's family — had been beaten until the men signed the papers saying they volunteered to give up everything they owned and leave.

In the mall where his family would soon open the restaurant, Baba said. "What is a bike worth?"

"Hajurba's bike?" Samir didn't think he meant the dollar price.

"Yes."

"He said Hajurama would be impressed that he has such a good bike."

"And soon he will have a better one because of this business."

They walked.

"To make this business run," Baba said, "you need to help. You know more about these things. You have to help. You and Heera know what people want. You yourself work at an American restaurant."

Samir knew Ethel called the police if somebody gave her a bad credit card. She hollered the license plate numbers of people who ate and didn't pay into the police dispatcher. "You don't make the money, you're outta business. Nobody's stiffing me." Police were her regular customers. She gave the officers coffee and crullers for free and whipped through her photos to show her daughter with wild hair, and they showed her photos of their dogs.

Samir nodded. "I will help you," he said.

"Whatever is going on here, it is petty. This is a country of justice and laws," Baba said. "What happens among high-school boys is not worth fighting about. No bully is worth fighting. Try to find another way. You must avoid this problem. All the time, there is fighting in Nepal. Let it go here. You cannot fight here. No matter what. You understand?"

Samir wished he had fifty classmates to fight Gabe. He wanted to fight him so badly even if he failed.

"I understand, Baba. I will not."

21

OLIVE

In the back field at Gabe's house, Gabe and Olive were building a trellis for the climbing peas. They worked in the scent of the fresh-mown grass in the late afternoon. She left him doing some final work on the trellis and began harvesting greens for Julia to prepare for a market in Dover.

When she came back, the trellis was done. He'd left it leaning by the chicken house. Gabe, though, was sprawled on the grass under the sun, asleep.

She knew he'd been up the night before fishing on a groundfishing boat. And the day job at PowerSports today.

His chest rose and fell, deep sleep.

She lay on her back beside him. Under the clear sky, she could picture all the field around her by the woods where the owls called.

She propped herself up on her elbow. Gabe didn't wake up.

She pulled out her phone, checked email. Mr. Farley had sent a message: *Congratulations on your position as Counselor at the North Mersea Day Camp, City of Mersea, New Hampshire. This is a reminder: Thursday morning, 8 a.m. Counselors' Orientation and Training. Yours sincerely, Adam Farley.*

Mom would be ecstatic.

Olive clicked on Firefox. Then she searched Bhutan.

Bhutan, she read, was called Land of the Thunder Dragon. They had a king and they called the king's son the dragon prince. It was in the Himalayan mountains and it was landlocked. She remembered the dot on the map.

She clicked on more sites. She read that sometimes people kept livestock on the first floor of the house and the people lived on the floors above. She saw a photo of a small boy in a multicolored woven robe tied with a sash, bare knees, black knee socks, a cute grin. The dragon prince. He looked about four.

She pulled her hood over her head.

"Now I know," she whispered.

"What do you know?" Gabe said. He opened his eyes, groggily waking up. His eyes glittered in the sun. They did the slowest kiss and it was like they lived in a place eternal when they kissed.

She felt her phone by her far side. She knew Bhutan had a dragon prince.

"I know I can sleep out here," she said.

She stretched out and tried to focus on the sun searing her cheeks.

"Out here, everything is simple. Like you are very black

and white. You know what you're doing."

"I know what my father thinks I'm doing."

He turned to her on the warm, bumpy earth and grass on the hillside.

"I've heard it all my life. *You spend a couple years in the indoctrination factory, you sold your soul. Nothing for you there. Nothing for a white kid.* He's talking about college. He follows that stuff on talk shows. You hear it enough you believe it. He wants me to get a job at the shipyard."

He kept on talking, like she was the only person he could tell it to. Nobody at the bike shop. Nobody at home. There he was just God.

"My father has to keep working. What is he, nearly sixty? Hasn't got a dime. He's climbing these twenty-foot ladders. He won't see a doctor. People aren't calling him up for jobs so much 'cause he looks fucking sick."

"There's something I'm not sure of about him."

"Nothing about him you don't know."

"Yeah, but we promised we'd never not tell each other what's on our mind. So we don't bury things. We have to always be able to talk."

"What's on your mind?" A crease cut in the skin between his eyebrows.

"The old man's bike."

"Jesus Christ."

"Are you mad at Kyle about that?" Olive asked.

"He didn't do shit with the bike."

"What do you mean? He threw the bricks in their window."

"Yeah, he did. That's it. But that bike was sitting half in the street like it was trash pickup. Like all the trash they keep over there. So I picked it up. Helped them get rid of it. Look, I just started this really grueling job and I'm trying to get it all right. Could you give me a break about your new buddies?"

"They're not my buddies."

Gabe was on his feet, crossing the field. "I keep thinking of you on the last day of school. The day I started my job."

"Everybody was celebrating." And then she remembered, she was going to ask Samir about the horse. The dancers were all around him. That's what Gabe saw. People liked Samir.

"I just don't want anything to change," he said. "I love you so goddamn much. I don't want you to change."

"I'm not changing. I'm right here." She ran to him and held his face and touched the dent above his lips. And then his beautiful straight lips. They were both almost crying.

"You scared me," he said.

"You scared me."

"Let's quit scaring each other," he said.

She wrapped her arms around his waist.

"I don't want to fuck this up. I want to marry you," he said.

"That's what I want, Gabe. I want to go to school, too, like you. Figure out how to get financial aid, even if it means going at least half time. We can figure this all out together."

Gabe put his hands in her hair and pulled her to his chest. She pulled him to the ground.

"I can't stand those people," he said.

He laid the blame on the government who didn't give a damn and gave everything to the immigrants. And the rich drug people. She was almost jealous of Gabe's certainty.

For some reason, she thought of the little rose in her garden from Geeta. What a silly name. And the old man.

She kept the picture he drew of the school on the island. They perplexed her, these people with strange stories and pictures of horses.

But above all things, she was loyal to her family — Mom and Gabe. Those people hurt Gabe. They hurt Olive.

She felt Gabe's body fit with hers.

"Okay, so here's my idea." She straddled him.

He reached up and kissed her eyes.

"Let's get out of here. Like Chris said. And we talked about. Get the fuck outta this place. It's hurting both of us here. Where does it say we have to stay here?"

"We both got jobs," he said.

"It's more than jobs. It's us. It's the lives we want with each other. It's like this place is tearing us apart."

"We don't have to let it," he said. "You want to graduate high school first?"

She could tell he was trying to be funny. As if any of this idea of moving was her being a child. And he thought everything they had was here.

"Maybe," she said. "But just think about it for a minute with me. What if we could always have each other if we didn't have all this? Wonder with me."

He was not that good at wondering.

"You remember the place. Way up in Maine on the lake. That town called Jackman where you and me and Chris were going. Brand-new place for a life. You brought it up first."

"I have a real job now."

"I do, too. Gabe, they're paying me $17 an hour because I have my lifesaving certificate."

"Olive, I can't do this."

"If we could imagine, what's one thing you'd take? I'd take my guitar."

"You're crazy."

"You know what else I'd take? Just imagine that we could go where we could always have each other. They've got these floats they strung up outside the Day Night. These dolphin floats for the tourists to take to the beach. I'd take one of those to the lake."

"I'll get you a dolphin float," he said. "We'll take it to the ocean. What do we want a lake for?"

"So we can run away. You're so bad at this game."

She had a distinct idea they were each talking about something different. She kept on with every physical thing they could fit in their backpacks. They wouldn't take much.

"The spoons Chris gave me when I was eleven. The Lord of the Rings, all of them. My Grecian green vase I made. The afghan my mom made —"

"Olive," he said. "There's only one thing I'd take, wherever. Whether it's upstairs in this rat of a house or some other place. You're the only thing I want. Just you."

Then he stood up and he pulled her up. "Why can't we have each other right here in Mersea?"

She rubbed her arms like there was a chill in the evening.

We're not safe here, she almost said. She was scared for them.

"Do you love me?" he said.

"I love you forever."

22

SAMIR

Before Samir could stop him, he heard Bhim rap loudly on Olive's front door. She came with water streaming down her face and neck. She wore sweats and dripping hair.

"How do you do this?"

Bhim held up a can opener the wrong way at the rim of a can of tuna. He looked up at her.

"How to open? You always have books."

Olive had *The Two Towers* in her hand.

"Come on, Bhai," Samir called.

"What does it say?" Bhim asked, grinning.

Olive asked, "Do you like books?"

Bhim nodded with serious eyes.

"Jum," Samir said sharply. "I'll open the can. Let's go." To Olive he said, "He keeps talking about you."

Bhim sang out, "He has a Ganesha. Did you see?"

Samir leaned down to him. "Let's go."

Bhim lifted the gold chain that Samir wore around his neck, and on the chain was a small gold pendant.

"See? Ganesha," Bhim told Olive. "Because he is smart. Ganesha is the lord of learning."

Olive stepped a little closer and squinted at the pendant. "An elephant?"

"Yes!" Bhim said.

Samir shoved the chain inside his shirt and grabbed Bhim's arm.

Suddenly Olive backed into the porch wall. She looked up the street.

Was she expecting Gabe? Or could he simply come at any time? She stepped back because she should not be seen looking at Samir's elephant.

Bhim wanted *her* to help with the can.

"Bhim, let's do it," she said. They set the can of tuna on the porch table. She took his hand and they hooked one part of the can opener beneath the rim of the can, pressed the blade into the top and twisted the crank. He cranked it himself.

"He just wanted to come over," Samir said. "I'm sorry if he is a problem."

When they finished, the oil of the tuna dripped down their fingers. Olive's cat appeared. It tried to rub its tail against Samir's leg, but Samir moved from it.

"You don't like cats," she said.

"They are witches," Bhim squealed.

"They told that in the camp," Samir said. "Some people

had folktales." He did not intend to be friendly and tell her things, such as about a cat. But it felt okay.

She scooped the cat up in her arms like it weighed no more than its hair. The cat reached to the scent of the oil. Samir touched its short stripes of orange, brown and white fur.

The girl was watching him. He hadn't talked to Olive since the day she walked his family to the ESL class.

"This is your third favor. The lawn mower, the streamers, the tuna-fish can."

He owed her one. The sound of Gabe's dirt bike had not come yet.

Olive said, "You're welcome!" and ran inside and he thought they were done. But she came back with a picture book.

"We have stacks of these," she told Bhim. "You can read it."

He opened it and saw a picture of a caterpillar. "Can I show Ama?"

"Yup." Olive squatted down to talk to him. "At my job — I started this morning — we look for bugs and crabs and caterpillars. You like bugs?"

"Butterflies!" he said.

She and Samir exchanged glances. Her eyes laughed.

Bhim held the storybook to his chest. Samir held the tuna and they crossed to the other side where the chickens pecked in the dirt around new yellow flowers.

Across the street, Hajurba wanted to ride far and Samir didn't want him to go alone, so he decided to run beside him.

"I'm coming, too," Bhim said.

"You can't. It's too far."

Hajurba led the way on the bike. Samir followed behind. They waved to Bhim.

They raced on a narrow bridge over the creek and into the woods. Hajurba was making this a long ride, over footbridges and trails that forked off each other. They entered a neighborhood Samir had never seen before. The streets were unpaved and new houses were being built.

Samir heard giggling behind him. He was about to go back when he saw the trail turn.

Hajurba was way ahead, standing in the backyard of the house where the trail ended. He was bending down over a large dog kennel carefully constructed of brown-painted boards. Hajurba walked all the way around it to see what might be inside.

Around the corner in the distance were two men working on the house beside a pallet of narrow, long boards. They measured the boards on a standing saw and cut the strips of wood to a correct length. The saw was loud and clicked on and off as they worked. The men handled the boards with such care that Samir thought this was an art to create these perfect boards to build the kinds of houses like the one he now lived in — carefully cut boards nailed on the inner boards.

In the camp, they lived in quickly built huts made of bamboo and plastic. Samir's grandfather was one of the people who wove the strips of bamboo to make a wall. He had no land of his own. In Bhutan, someone else lived in the strong farmhouse he and Hajurama built on the hillside. He had been twenty when they built it. She was sixteen.

The saw cut off.

"Come on," Samir told his grandfather. "This is their yard."

Hajurba was humming.

The men talked. They were arguing. Samir did not want to be there. They were at a distance, but then Samir knew these voices. He looked straight at them.

Gabe and his father. Samir had seen this man at the café. He wanted to say something so they knew they were there, to say they were just walking on the trail. Do not be alarmed.

But if he spoke, he would alarm them.

Gabe was talking to the older man. "Mom said you gotta get checked out. What happened?"

The father was nailing boards around the edges of a window.

"Gonna rain," he yelled back.

"Dad," Gabe called. "It's a doctor's appointment."

"Not gettin' in any fucking gaymobile." He kept his back to his son. He hammered the boards onto the house with solid, sure hits. He was old but he had muscles in his shoulders and back. "You gotta break free. You're *white* people," he hollered. "You need some moral toughness. You always did."

"Dad," Gabe said, "I'm getting you some help." But Samir imagined the shame in his eyes like he saw that day at the River's Tale. Samir knew the shame or fear of shame, if he didn't live up to what his father thought his son should be.

"You can't trust strangers for your health." That was the father. Then something about a hospital like a prison and your wife has to sign a socialist paper to get you out. The voices turned on and turned off as they worked.

Then for some reason Samir could not fathom, the father and son had their hands on each other's shoulders, and they started to circle like they were kids wrestling. Samir realized Gabe was trying to get his father in his car, but the father would not go. They kept circling and the father threw a jab at Gabe.

Gabe's voice was low but he was talking all the time while he ducked.

"They're not putting you in the hospital." Gabe shouted that.

This time the father wrapped his elbow around his son's neck and forced him into a hold with Gabe's arm twisted behind his upper back. The old man grimaced as he gripped his son. Samir knew this domination move in martial arts. It hurt to watch. But maybe it was that the boy would not fight the man.

The father let him go and laughed, but Gabe didn't. Samir couldn't hear what they said.

He heard the father yell, "Christ sake, use your head. Who's gonna pay the bills? College? That's not paying. That's taking handouts so you pay the government the rest of your life."

The father left his son and moved on to the next window.

Gabe paced. Samir and Hajurba stood back by the trees mostly hidden.

Gabe ripped his own shirt over his head and threw it on the ground. Then he lifted a board. He angled it so he could move the board through the blade, then carried it to the corner of the house where he held it beside a window. His father nailed it in place at the top, the center, the bottom.

They did not talk anymore. They sawed and nailed as if this was something they had done many times. This is what they did well.

It was only when Hajurba mounted the bike and began to pedal, and the loud saw was quiet, that they were discovered. The stones scattered and the bike lurched. Hajurba put one foot to the stones to keep from falling.

The man and Gabe were startled and turned fast to the trail.

Just then, Samir heard the giggling again, closer. This time he saw. It was the last person who should be here. Bhim.

"Stop!" he shouted.

Bhim had not heard Samir shout before, and he froze.

Then an explosion of voices.

"Get the fuck off this property. You're trespassing." The father had his phone out. "Calling the cops."

The men pounded across the dirt and weeds of the land.

"My grandfather wandered off the trail," Samir said. "We're just going by."

Samir and Hajurba turned the bike around. They moved but the trees didn't shield them from anything.

"You're fucking way off the trail," Gabe shouted.

Samir and Gabe were now a few yards apart. Gabe was half a head taller. The sun glinted through the trees above him.

Samir imagined himself smashing Gabe's jaw.

Gabe didn't shout, but his voice was strong and carried. "I'll tell you one more time. Stay away from me. Stay away from Olive. Leave her family alone. The little kid." He pointed at Bhim who had stopped where he was in his red T-shirt in the middle of the trail. "That old man. All of you, don't you dare come near any of my people."

Samir turned back, his body rigid. Gabe could attack Samir, but not his brother or his grandfather.

But if you're going to fight — this is what Hajurba always said — *do not show your fear.*

Gabe dropped his voice lower. "If I ever see you or that old man creeping around my father's worksite, the owners are going to press charges against you." Gabe kept his voice low and calm and threatening. "Stealing, attempted break-in, vandalism. They'll throw the book at you."

The father hung over a concrete slab, coughing hard. It looked like splats of blood on the ground. It was a convulsing cough.

Gabe stepped back to him. "It's cool. Everything's cool," he said to his dad. He turned hard-faced to Samir. "Beat it." He swore and spat out a string of slurs before he turned, and Samir fisted his hands and leapt toward him.

Hajurba laid his hand on Samir's back. "Not now. Not with the boy. We will get him home."

The three continued on the trail, Hajurba upright on his bike, Samir taking his time, holding firmly to Bhim's hand.

"There they go," the father yelled after the fit of coughs stopped. "There's your replacement." His voice was raspy and weak.

Hajurba and Samir didn't talk on the way home. Bhim kept turning to look behind them.

"Why did they call us Irani? Are we Irani? What is Chink?"

"They don't know what they're talking about," Samir said. He was shaking and tried to quiet himself so Bhim wouldn't understand. "They were just loud, rowdy workmen. They have nothing to do with us."

"No, they were yelling at me. Why are they angry?"

"You did nothing. Don't worry."

Samir watched his grandfather's straight back as his legs pumped the pedals.

At home, Bhim could not stop telling about the men in the woods.

Bhim asked Auntie, "Why did they tell me to stay away? What did I do? Ching chong," Bhim began. He had to think. "Curry-muncher. Pajeet."

And then Bhim said to Auntie and later Baba, "Samir almost hit a boy. He made giant fists to get ready to hit him, but then he didn't. But it's good he didn't, because the boy would have beat him up."

Samir found out that the story wasn't even going to be a secret to the neighbors. Soon Bhim got on the bike with streamers, as he did whenever he could get the bike, and rode up Olive's short driveway and knocked on her door.

"What does it mean to throw the book. They said they'd throw the book at us."

He held his arms to his chest like he held the book about butterflies Olive had lent him.

"Who said that to you?"

"Your friend. That boy."

"Gabe?"

"He said I should keep away from you and Hajurba should keep away. He said he'd call the police on us."

"Come home," Samir shouted at Bhim from across the street. "Now!"

"Where?" Olive asked. Her voice was high-pitched.

"In the woods. They were building a house."

"Oh, God," Olive said.

Then Bhim had to tell her everything. The wrestling. The bad words.

"And that man!" Bhim's eyes were wide. "He was so mad, he coughed up blood. Why is he mad at me?"

Olive bent down to him. When Samir approached to take his hand, Bhim shouted, "And they almost had a fight!"

"Who?" Olive said. "Did you and Gabe get into it?"

"Come!" Samir took Bhim by the hand. He did not want this conversation with her.

Olive stood up. "Gabe wouldn't do that."

Bhim said, "He did."

Samir didn't look at Olive. He picked Bhim up and carried the boy who was now crying and the bike and took them home.

23

OLIVE

Olive sat rigid on the front stoop. She had sat there for at least half an hour after Bhim left.

Her mother stepped out on the porch.

"Get the mower."

"Why now?"

"Grass needs cutting. Julia's coming."

Julia?

Slowly Olive crossed the street. The Paudels' fence leaned in and out like a ribbon on its edge. She did not want to disturb anyone, especially Samir. She didn't want to believe the story Bhim had sung out. But she did. She could tell Samir didn't want to talk to her.

Olive saw the chicken house, the spindly lilac tree, the tumble of lobster traps. She went around back where the lawn mower might be, taking a narrow path that led into an open space she hadn't known was there. The back door was open and inside she could see their kitchen and hear them talk. Outside were flowers and sprouts of green in the large garden. From their door, they'd hung something like a clothesline with bright-colored triangles of fabric flying in the wind.

That's when she saw the window. It was ugly beside the flowers and bright cloth. They had tried to keep the glass from falling in with strips of duct tape and then tried to bag it in black plastic that had come loose and flapped.

Olive imagined what she and Mom would have done if they were making breakfast and somebody threw bricks at their kitchen window. They'd get the cops there in a heart-beat. She saw on the news how a man broke into a house with a hammer because he hated the person who lived inside.

Olive passed the window. No lawn mower. She stomped up the front porch stairs, startled the chicken sitting on a wicker chair. She stumbled over rows of flip-flops and sandals.

"Hello! It's me, Olive."

Silence. She saw Ms. Geeta through the mesh of the screen but she didn't come out.

Bhim opened the front door. He came with the butterfly book and asked her to read.

"You want me to read to you?"

"Yes." He looked tired.

She squatted down on the grass with him at the far end of the porch where she could still see the flapping plastic at the back of the house.

A willow tree hung its boughs over the traps. Ms. Geeta came out. She was unsmiling as ever but, for a moment, she knelt on the ground and touched Olive's face. Her fingertips were fine sandpaper.

"Did you call a glass company to fix your window?" Olive said, when she really wanted to ask how Samir was. Was he angry?

Ms. Geeta said something in Nepali. Olive mumbled, "Gabe shouldn't have done that, the things Bhim said."

Just then she heard a scream or a shout from across the street, from her own house. It was her mother.

"I'm coming!" Olive shouted.

Bhim had Olive's hand when she started to run from the house. He tried to interlace his fingers with hers.

"My mom," she cried out. She pulled her hand, and it slipped away with their sweat in the humid air. Why did the little boy trust her?

Then from the corner of her eye, she saw the KTM orange flash by. *Gives you wings* embroidered on the rider's back. The bumper sticker *America Is Full Go Home.*

Gabe was here.

Gabe and Olive found Mom at the same time. She had not fallen down or sliced open her head or electrocuted herself. She was standing at the kitchen stove with a metal spatula in her hand. She was frying chicken like she used to. She'd quartered potatoes and put them on to boil and Olive smelled garlic and she saw Mom was making her special garlic mashed potatoes. She wore a T-shirt that said she loved cats.

"What's going on, Mom?"

"Almost time," she called, as if this was a usual meal for them to eat together, and that was the reason she'd screamed out.

Gabe dropped into the old oak rocker they kept in the kitchen.

"I wanted to cook for you kids."

It was weird. They hadn't all come to eat together in a long time. Olive couldn't look at him.

Then Julia and Simone called from the door.

Julia hugged Mom and they all eased into kitchen work, clanging plates on the table, stirring pots on the stove, sliding the biscuits out of the oven.

"You got a garden going?" Julia said. She'd opened the back door. And there in the dirt was the rose plant.

Her mother's eyes laughed and seemed bigger tonight, like she'd become related to the round moon. The world was sad, but look, we have this. That's what Olive saw in Mom's calm, open eyes.

"Did you start it?" Julia asked.

"I didn't," Mom said.

But she didn't tell her that Geeta used her hands and pictures on her phone to show how she started the plant from hips.

Olive wanted to escape. This could not be normal. That they could not tell the truth about the rose. That a boy could be two people. The gentle boy who cherished her. And a boy who could probably set the neighbor's house on fire.

Inside, the smell of chicken frying was like so many befores. Mom placed a vase of sprawling mountain laurel on the table and petals dropped on the plates. Gabe put on the funny flowered apron hanging behind the door and whisked milk into the chicken drippings for gravy, added a shake of flour, and the whisk tinged against the skillet. Gabe mixed up the ingredients carefully, winking at his little sister who came to whisk with him.

When they sat down to eat, the chicken dropped off the bone into their mouths. The batter was fried crisp and they made wells in the mashed potatoes with the backs of their forks and filled the wells with Gabe's gravy. Julia said if she shut her eyes, she'd be back in Georgia.

Olive tried to let her body release like the cat who sprawled in the sun. She glanced at Gabe's large, deft hands as he ate. He winked at her.

He was totally calm and sweet. He was Olive's family. She wondered if he was part of the calmness in her mother's eyes, the steadiness of Gabe. Olive tried to see his face contorted in rage while he shouted racial slurs at the neighbors.

Mom said, "All we need is butter and sugar corn. That'll come ripe in July and go on all summer."

Mom talked about the women in the jail. Today they painted cards for their kids.

"They haven't been sentenced yet," she said. "They still get up at 5:30, wash the sleep out of their eyes, brush their teeth, eat their breakfast like groggy teenagers."

"Grace of God, you'll dodge going to jail," Julia said to Olive and Simone, to warn them about the world.

Olive glanced at her. "Those girls. From what Mom's described, I think people can only bear to lose so much."

"That's just what one girl said today," Mom said. "She weeps when she talks about being separated from her baby."

The sun came out. It was low and pale and hung over the street. ·

Then a police car rolled along Chestnut Street. Mom watched.

"I've seen them ride by now and then," Mom said, "since the incident across the street."

There was a beat of silence. Then Simone said, "Gabe is king of the bike shop."

"Whoa," he laughed. "Of the parts department. Largest inventory of bike parts in the Northeast."

Mom was still looking out the window.

"You grab the mower?" she asked Olive.

Olive shook her head.

"Where is it?" Gabe asked. "I'll get it."

Her heart clenched.

They'd lasted through supper, and no one had brought up the lawn mower or someone smashing the neighbor's window or stealing their bike because they hated the people inside. Or the cursing at Mr. Paudel and a little boy. All of them around the table had surprised each other with the ease of eating together. They were an old, gnarled family with holes like the knot-holed table at Gabe's house.

"Just tell me where," Gabe said.

Olive looked at his freckles. They popped in the sun. He stood and she could see he almost put his arms around her.

"It's across the street at Samir's house. Theirs didn't work."

"How'd it get there?" His eyes fixed on hers and she almost flinched. His eyes were wide and the blue darkened. They changed as quick as it took to say Samir's name.

"I rolled it over."

"Jesus Christ," he said through his teeth, just like his father.

"It's not a problem," Olive said. "I can get it."

"It's a problem," he said sharply.

"Their old one started and died. It was to give us some peace."

"What would you know about giving somebody some peace?" Gabe's voice was deep and low and hard.

The whole family stopped talking and stared at Olive and Gabe.

Olive was so startled she said, "Stop blasting me! Stop it. And since when do you need to tell somebody to stay away from my house?"

"I'm not blasting anybody. You're full of accusations. If you can dish it, you got to be able to take it, Olive."

"You screamed insults at a little boy. Gabe, he's like, five."

Simone swooped in to grab hold of her brother's arm.

"I want to go home, Gabe. Let me ride with you on the bike!"

But Gabe turned to Olive again.

"I trusted you," he said low and very slowly, and he strode out with Simone, her hair flowing like a curtain.

Mom was at the table picking chicken off the bones.

"This was supposed to be a party."

Olive ran up the stairs. Slammed her door. Put on her headphones and blasted "Make My Day" on repeat, shut her eyes and tore around her room. Hard and fast, blasting the words with Coi Leray. She built up a good, slippery sweat.

Make my day. Make my day.

Then she lightly came downstairs. Opened the screen door.

"Mom, I'm getting the lawn mower."

She let the screen door slam.

24

SAMIR

Auntie spoke loudly, like she always did. Here, away from his larger family, Samir was aware that Nepali people talked louder than Americans.

Still, her voice sounded even louder than usual.

Auntie was talking on the phone to Ama.

Samir and Hajurba sat on the floor on either side of the carrom board. Hajurba loved playing carroms. He played all the time in Pathri. Now they sat with the black and white pieces surrounding the red queen in the center of the black-and-white board. They took turns flicking the striker.

Auntie kept talking about the incident this afternoon.

Samir repeated to them, "Nothing happened. By accident we walked on somebody's property. Hajurba was looking at their dog kennel. They didn't like it. And we left. That's it."

Baba and Uncle would come soon, they'd all explain again. But Bhim would be asleep, so Samir would tell the story.

Samir spoke softly to his grandfather. "You know what happened today?"

"La," Hajurba said, not looking up from the board.

"This boy is causing me problems. I want to get him in trouble. I want to vandalize his bike. I want to fight him."

Hajurba kept his gaze on the board. He flicked the striker.

"La," Hajurba said in a breathless way because he missed this one.

"I cannot talk to Baba," Samir said. "This person is out to get me. Baba says no fighting."

Samir worried that he should not have laid this burden down. His grandfather could do nothing, and now he was sad. Maybe he would talk to Baba about moving to Nebraska. Samir thought now he would lecture on the golden ball of fire. *Have you swallowed it?* Yes. *Now feel your power radiate to all parts of you.*

But he didn't. It was Samir's turn and he flicked the striker. He missed the second one.

"La," Hajurba said. "For bullies, you must have seven friends. How many friends do you have?"

Samir looked at Hajurba like he had maybe lost his mind, or simply could not understand what Samir was saying.

It was true he, himself, was prideful and friendless. But he had hoped for instruction on using his discipline, his strength, his grit to be a better fighter like Hajurba had been in his youth.

"I don't mean about friends," Samir said. "I mean about fighting."

"Seven friends," Hajurba repeated.

"I have many friends from Pathri. They are in cities everywhere. Many cities."

"Friends here," Hajurba said. His narrow fingers had perfect aim and sank piece after piece. He had been a carrom player in Pathri, though not as superior as Bishnu. "How many friends do you have?"

"None," Samir said. "But I am strong. You told me once, do not show your fear. Tell me how to do that like you did when you used to fight."

"La," Hajurba said after he flicked the striker. "Well, when you have seven friends, then you will have no bully."

"Hajurba, I can't make friends in Mersea. You don't understand."

Hajurba showed no mercy or sorrow. "Everywhere are bullies and people who hate you. So first you must have friends."

Samir was completely exasperated. When he got a turn, he hit the striker too hard and the piece bounced off the board.

Auntie got off the phone. Then everybody was talking loudly in the living room. First they discussed the window. They were tired of the black plastic flapping in the wind, but Baba was too busy.

"We must replace the window." Auntie began to google in Nepali how to put a glass pane in the window. She would do it. They would not wait anymore for Baba or Uncle.

Hajurba had hung the peace flags to safeguard the garden they were preparing. Now he said, "I will paint a good-luck swastika for the front door."

"In America it is bad," Auntie said to Hajurba. "If a person draws one, police will come and say they have committed a crime."

Hajurba said the smashed window was a worse crime than a good-luck Nepali swastika, like the one Buddha had on his foot. To Hindus it was a good sign. Here they had freedom of religion.

Samir walked a tightrope. He must calm his family. Baba had tried to report the cracked window to the police. Bishnu would say the worst thing is for police to come. People must handle problems among the family.

Samir did not have things under control.

Later, he talked with Ama. She asked if he was all right. He repeated that he was fine. It was just like Worcester. It was just like any place. People had arguments.

He was lying and afraid.

Then Heera got the phone. "Sometimes I think we should have stayed in Nepal."

"Nepal didn't want us."

"I know that, but we're young. Maybe we would have hidden in the city and proven ourselves and we could have made Kathmandu our home."

"There was no place for the elders. They would have died in the camp or the city. Here is home."

"My home is my family," Heera proclaimed. "I would like everyone in the family to please come to live with us when Ama and I come to New Hampshire."

"Heera, I have to go."

"What is it?"

"Someone is at the door."

They all heard the insistent sound of knocking.

Samir looked out and saw a police car pulled up along their fence.

Baba wasn't home. Samir would have to talk to them. Why now? Had someone heard the shouting in the woods? Did someone call the police? Everyone would know the man who rode a yellow bike around the village.

Nothing had happened. That's what he would say. He knew they had driven by since the morning Baba called. But they had not knocked on the door.

He did not know if the police coming was good or bad. What he needed, he decided, was seven friends. He wasn't hopeful with this advice. But he would begin with finding one.

25

OLIVE

Olive ran down her porch steps and across to Samir's yard. Dead quiet.

This time she saw the push mower at the far end of the porch beneath the eaves. She ran across the yard and was just about to spin the mower around when the police cruiser pulled up on Samir's side of the road and two police officers strode up the path.

"Who are you?" It was the first cop, who was a woman.

"Just the neighbor. They borrowed our lawn mower."

The officer's eyes slid to the lawn mower.

"I was taking it home. I live over there." She pointed to her house.

"Stay here," the officer said. "I'd like to ask some questions."

"Okay." Olive froze.

Both officers climbed the porch steps. They knocked.

Then another car pulled into the driveway, and a man she thought was Samir's father jumped out, as well as another man. They walked quickly to the porch, right past Olive.

The father introduced himself to the police at the same time that Samir opened the door.

The police said they were in the Neighborhood Patrol Program and asked how they were doing. They said they wanted to follow up on the complaint Mr. Paudel had called in.

But the father wanted to speak first. He spoke formally, holding his hands in front of his chest and moving them as if he were holding a wiggling baby.

"We are a family business. We want to open our new business. We do not wish to bring trouble to this city."

Then he introduced each member of the family, who must have been somewhere behind him. "My son. My father. My sister. My brother. Also, he is my brother. This is his young son."

The other man Olive had seen spoke in Nepali and nudged Samir in the chest.

Then Samir told the officer what the man was saying.

"Thank you for coming. We understand this makes your city uneasy. We will fix the window."

"We are fine," the man said in English. Bhim did not tell the cops about the almost-fight in the woods. He watched them all with wide eyes.

One cop went to look around. The other cop — the

woman — stayed at the door with the family. She talked very low and she gave the father a piece of paper.

"Vandalizing your house is illegal. At best, they want to frighten you. At worst, they want to hurt you."

Samir spoke something in Nepali. Olive wondered if he changed her meaning so his family wouldn't be frightened.

"Think about putting up a security camera."

Samir told that to the family. Most people were now on the porch. They nodded to her.

"We'll just have a look at the window," she said.

The woman cop walked through a bunch of shoes toward Olive at the end of the porch, still with her hands on the mower. She seemed barely older than Lise and Olive. She wore her dark hair twisted at the back of her neck. Her name tag said *Byatt*.

"You're the neighbor." Officer Byatt came down the steps to Olive. "What's your name?"

"Olive Ronan."

"You see anybody around this yard?"

"Just them." She pointed to the red porch. "They have a kid and he plays out here."

The officer gave Olive a card, too.

"If you or your parents see something, call me. I want to talk to your parents. You mind giving me your address and phone?"

Olive did that. Why didn't the cops give her a card when Chris was finding stuff with fentanyl on the streets and say, *You see something, call me.* Why didn't they protect him?

The other officer strode across the grass where Olive had seen Samir dance. They found the narrow path and followed it the way Olive had, and they'd see the window as well as the row of flying flags.

Samir's father and Bhim went with them. Olive heard their voices. Then the officers got in the cruiser, pulled away from the house and inched down the street toward the Day Night, holding up the cars behind them.

Olive pushed the mower across the grass. Then for some reason she didn't know, she sat down on a wooden stool the Paudels used as a lawn chair. She took in the whole little yard, the yellow light from her own kitchen that shone in the dim light through Samir's leaning fence, and down the hill to the Day Night sign rising up.

Anger socked Olive in the face. Anger about the stupid window. About their bike in the creek. Anger at the beauty of Samir's dance. That enraged her.

Anger about how a brother who won her a set of spoons at the county fair could overdose one day in the garage with his dirt bike disassembled all around him and she and Gabe couldn't start his breathing again. Anger that was Gabe when he looked at Samir Paudel.

Did anger sock Samir in the face about Mr. Paudel's yellow bike? About Gabe treating him like shit?

The door opened and clicked shut. He didn't even slam it.

Samir stepped barefoot down the porch steps. His cap nearly covered his eyes.

"I do not want to be rude, but you have to go home."

She stood.

Around them she heard a baby crying, the click of a car engine that wouldn't turn over. She imagined a fistful of the jail women's crochet needles clicking.

"Okay."

She stepped back to the fence. She stood in her holey jeans and her angry sticks of hair.

She made fists with her hands.

"Why aren't you angry? About Gabe. What he said."

"Why are you angry?" His voice was still calm. His face had no expression. But there was something like fear in his hands. He held them clasped tight.

"You have a sister," she said. "You said you talk to her."

"I talk to her four times every day."

"Four times?"

"We are very close."

"What do you talk about?"

He shrugged. "Nothing much. Just what we are doing. It is a comfort."

"She's your sister. Why doesn't she live here?"

"My mother is finishing her course. Then they'll come. My family is opening a restaurant here."

He had more family than Olive.

"You said your brother left. Do you talk to him?" Samir asked.

She looked at the garage. She almost told him about Chris.

"What is your family going to do?" Olive put her hand on the gate.

"In August my mother and Heera are coming to live here."

"Heera is your sister?"

"You need to go. If someone sees you here, it could be more trouble for my family."

He meant Gabe.

Although he told her to leave, he kept talking. "I am a mystery to Americans. Muslim? No. Mexican? No. Asian? Where is Tibet? Bhutan, I never heard. So people try to guess what I am. None are acceptable."

Olive almost asked, *So what are you?*

"Your rap. You said you were from Bhutan."

"Nepal," he said.

"Oh," she said.

"Maybe you have heard of Mount Everest."

"Tibet."

"Near there."

Then he seemed to hesitate. He had told her to go. But he was looking at her as if he were weighing his options.

"There is one thing," he said.

She dropped her hand from the gate.

"I don't know how to swim. I want to teach my sister. I want you to teach me."

"When do you want to?" she said.

"After work. Tomorrow. When can you come?"

"Three."

"I will come at three."

"It takes more than one time," she said.

"Okay," he said. "Two times. Where the horse whistles."

"There's a current. It flows hard to the ocean."

"I am a dancer. I'm strong."

"Didn't Gabe tell you not to talk to me?" Olive said.

"Yes."

She watched him and his face changed, as if a worry crossed his mind.

Then he asked, "He wouldn't hurt you, would he?"

"Hurt me?" she whispered. "You don't know him. You don't know one thing." She had her hand on the gate. "Look," she said. "Gabe and I are together. Never insult him."

"I just want to learn to swim," Samir said.

But then she paused. "Did he hurt you?"

"No."

His hair fell over his eyes in the street light. Sometimes he had a fierce attitude. Now he just seemed like any kid, even if he was from the Himalayas. A kid who wanted to swim. She was the most unlikely teacher. Gabe's girlfriend. But she could keep him from drowning and that wasn't bad. His dark eyes gleamed through his hair. He looked shy and graceful and awkward, too.

"All right," she said.

"All right. Good night."

She didn't know what made her say this, but she said, "I talk to my brother four times a day, too."

In the morning, on her first camp day with kids, Olive found Mom on the rickety bench in the garden. Mom wore her jail uniform. Olive wore her summer uniform — bathing suit, shorts, and she had a red scarf knotted on her head.

"How can you hate somebody and love somebody at the same time," Olive said, leaning her knee on the wheelbarrow, her pack on her shoulder.

Upstairs she had an overnight bag. It had been packed for two weeks, when she and Gabe first planned that she'd spend weekends. The bag was on her bed. A nightie, undies, a toothbrush.

Mom gazed up at her. Mom with the big eyes.

"Gabe is freaked out. At the neighbor."

"Kyle had an accident," Mom said. "He was driving that old truck. You know, the green and beige hunk of metal. He was going to a job yesterday and passed out. Ran the truck over a curb. Luckily it stalled and he didn't hit anybody."

"Was he drunk?"

She shrugged. "Julia says he's sick. He won't go to the doctor."

"Maybe that's why Gabe went off on me yesterday," Olive said.

Mom pressed her lips together. "He's loyal to his father," she said.

"I'm sixteen," Olive said. "My brother died. But I love a boy and a boy loves me. It's so simple."

So why was the overnight bag on her bed making her stomach ache?

In the main hall of the North Mersea Day Camp, Olive met the children in her group. They did skits to help them remember rules for the environment. Then they sat down at round tables with bowls of muffins in the middle that took forever to pass to kids who were five years old, Olive's group. They spread jelly on their muffins and then the muffins fell in their laps. Olive was paired with Jennifer to be her counselor partner.

Jennifer got the first-aid kit. They sang camp songs. Five

little speckled frogs sat on a speckled log eating the most delicious bugs yum yum.

Finally they were set free with instructions and collecting bags for a nature treasure hunt.

Natalie, Ben, April and Theodore trudged into the woods with Olive.

Bhim would really like this camp, Olive thought. They started off together at the tidal pool.

"At high tide," Olive told them information from her training, "this breakwater's a dam." She ran down stone steps to the wall of stones across the creek. "Look," she sang up to everyone while she stood wide-legged on the wall. "It breaks the water. It holds the water in. The pool rises and it becomes almost still at slack tide. The sun warms it. It kind of holds your body and you float."

"You float?" a little girl said.

"We won't. But we'll come every day to see how big the tidal pool is."

As Olive ran up the stone stairs, she saw the tidal pool was a beautiful deep forest green.

At the main hall again, everyone tried to remember the bird songs and sang them and showed their treasures.

They had a big messy lunch out on the rocks by the water. Olive checked her phone.

Text from Gabe. "Call me."

She didn't, then, in the middle of keeping the children out of the water. But something released inside her to see his name come up. She held the phone in both hands. Some kids were doing drumming and the sound of their drums pulsed through the trees. There was a messy picnic, and the last hour was for either arts and crafts, song fest or shore walk where you go with a bucket for shells or stones or whatever washed up in the sand.

But soon camp was done and the parents came, and kids clambered into their cars, and the counselors cleaned up in the main hall and planned the craft they'd do Monday. The camp ran from eight till two, Monday, Wednesday and Friday. She didn't make anything like Gabe was making. She planned to pitch in at home and at Gabe's if she stayed out there a lot.

She went to sit on a mossy rock in the quiet above the tidal pool. Below was the breakwater she'd shown the kids.

She got out her phone. Gabe again. He sent a video. He said he loved her.

She hit play. It was a dude explaining what happened to people's jobs when illegal immigrants came. He said salaries drop 30 percent for American workers.

"Immigrants get benefit checks and, most important, medical care that Americans don't get. Walls work! We've got to protect our borders," the man in the video said. "We know they smuggle in drugs like fentanyl that are killing —"

Olive clicked off the phone.

Her head hurt. She was about to jump into the green water below. Maybe she would float and maybe everything would stop.

But then she remembered. She was supposed to be at the cove. She was supposed to teach Samir to swim.

She got on her bike and raced like a coyote, and the wind was relief on her neck.

26

SAMIR

Samir was afraid of the water. Twice he left the cove. But then came back. Olive was already there. He could see her. She'd come like she said she would. She was focused on the horse that he could see across the water on the island.

In the wet sand, Olive drew the curve of a horse's back. She drew the outline of his mane, his flying feet, his nose. It was like the horse he drew on the whiteboard.

He heard her call out, "Hey, Lord of the Fishes."

She prepared to swim while Samir still huddled on the beach, his arms crossed and rubbing his hands up and down them.

That's when he climbed the tree between the woods and the shore. It was an apple tree with bark like scales that cut his legs. But he liked to be high and he could see far across the water in two directions.

Olive splashed into the water. She dove under. When she surfaced, he saw how her arms pulled through the water. He wanted to swim those strong strokes. He had watched a video that explained swimming built a muscular midsection, and those muscles connected the strong legs to the back and shoulders.

He was strong, but swimming would make him stronger.

He wasn't sure, though, if he could get in the water.

Olive circled around and swam back toward the shore. Then she stretched out on her back and she looked up into the sun and the trees.

That's when she spotted him. She stared at him and he stared at her through the branches.

Finally, she called to him. "You don't scare me."

"I wasn't trying to scare you." He stretched out on the limb of the knobby tree.

She swam in and scrambled out of the water. "You're like a tiger. But tigers can't climb trees."

"Yes, they do, very well," Samir called. "But they don't like to."

"Are you looking for Gabe? He's not here."

I can fight him, Samir wanted to assure her. In one agile move, he dropped to the ground. *But I don't want to.*

"I don't have much time," she said.

"I have watched how you swim. I practice it in my mind. I'm ready," he said to the river. It looked so easy when she glided onto her back. "But I don't want to feel the water."

"Pretty soon you won't feel it," she said.

When he put his toes still in flip-flops in the water, he

gasped. The horse whinnied to them and the sound pierced the wind.

"Listen," she said. "You can still hear his call like an echo."

For a second they listened to the sound that kept coming.

"You call him Lord of the Fishes?"

"Yes, he's lord of everything that swims."

"So this cove," Samir said. "It's his, too. It's Lord of the Fishes Cove."

They looked across the water. "And I'm going to swim in it."

"Okay," she said. "Let's do lesson one."

"Yes, lesson one." Samir put a whole foot in the water. "Ohhhhh," he called out. "But first I will show you my symbol."

"Look, why do you say you want to swim?"

"Because I have to help my sister swim. No one in my family knows how to swim."

Then beside Olive's horse in the sand, Samir drew a figure. He drew two legs leaping, arms wide reaching toward the sky. A curve for a head. That's all. But it made her laugh. Such happiness in the way the legs were flying.

"Okay, let's go!"

"Yes," he exclaimed, but he hesitated.

"Do you want to take off some of your clothes?"

She pointed at his flip-flops and the button shirt he still wore. Olive tied her T-shirt up under her breasts, which made him drop his eyes. The girls did not show so much of their body in his family.

She ran down to the water, maybe to give him privacy to do whatever Nepali people did.

He faced the tree and took off his shirt.

Olive jumped into the rolling waves.

Samir approached the water and pushed his feet against it like it was a wall of stones.

He inched out deeper.

Olive said, "Try to forget how cold the water is. Learning how to swim is about breathing."

"Breathing, yes." Samir wheezed in some air.

Olive's back was to the water. She kept an eye on him.

"You have a prince of your country?" she asked.

"There is a young prince today. Hajurba likes to tell stories about the old prince. His name is Jigme Khesar Namgyel Wangchuck. He is the fifth king. He graduated from high school in America."

"Where?"

"In Massachusetts. It was before I was born."

Samir's feet were so cold they ached. His shoulders quavered.

They splashed their way out.

"We won't go too far," she said. "See, the tide's halfway in, halfway to the highwater mark."

He waded in slow motion out to his hips. Even his face shook. He gritted his teeth and rolled his shoulders in so they almost touched his chin.

He said, "I swim. I swim."

"We can keep going like this, but it hurts less if you just get it over with. Like this."

Olive dropped under the blue-gray water. To him it was as cold as winter in the summer sun. She came up a few feet away.

"How can I? The water goes in the nose."

"No, you don't breathe when you go under. You hold your breath."

They practiced standing and holding their breaths for the count of one, two, three. Then she took a breath in, held it, dropped under, one, two, three, and popped up. She did this twice.

He would, too. He bent his knees and in slow motion, by sheer will, he descended.

"Now take in a breath before you go under and hold it."

When his face reached the water, he forced himself to submerge, but he took a breath in that instant and inhaled a lot of the salt water.

He leapt into the air, coughing, wheezing, gasping, shaking, lurching to shore. He bent over, hands to his knees, coughing the river water. He flashed back to the day on the edge of the waves when Gabe shoved him backwards.

He needed to learn how to breathe with the water.

"In August the water warms up," she called. He stopped choking. He sat cross-legged on the beach between two scrubby pines, his chest draped over his knees.

"I am relaxing my throat. I've been watching YouTube."

Olive laughed as she rose out of the river.

Samir stood. "You're laughing at me."

"No." She stood, one foot on a tree stump, bent over with laughter.

At first he was embarrassed about his swimming. Then he laughed and pounded his chest in glory. He had gone under.

"I should have told you to hold your nose," Olive laughed.

"It's your fault," he agreed.

"Lesson one is holy awful."

The tide was closer. Water lapped over her horse and Samir's lonely dancer and splashed over their feet and up to their ankles. He forced himself to withstand the cold of the water, then he ran splashing into the waves and Olive was still laughing and Samir made a big circle of flying water as he ran.

"We have a movie," Samir shouted to her. "It is called *Makkhi*. I am pretending I am Makkhi! He is a fly. In the movie he nosedives in the water and he never crashes."

"A fly?"

"Yes, a fly. I am Makkhi!" He opened his arms and stormed a breaker bar.

Across the way the horse was running and they ran up the beach, leaping over tree stubs and rocks and whooping with the crying gulls and into the tide that broke on the shore.

"Just in case, do you have a phone?"

"No one is too poor to have a phone."

"I didn't mean you were poor."

"A phone is the first thing we get in the camp."

It occurred to him she had a whole other world in her mind and he had his own. They entered each other's numbers in their phones. That was something they both had.

When Samir looked up, he saw two girls at the fork of the path. They carried a pail and maybe they were coming to collect shells or sea glass or other little things he had seen on the sand.

One had straight blonde hair to her waist.

"Simone!" Olive called out.

The girl stopped and looked at Olive with little blue angry eyes.

"Simone!" Olive called again.

But the girl ran away with her friend. She had hair like Heera's, except it was blonde.

"Who was that?" he said.

"Gabe's sister," Olive said. She had stopped running and stood breathing hard, and the laughter was gone from her face.

Samir knew the bond between a brother and a sister. She would tell him.

Olive began to pack her things.

She checked her phone. "I'm late. I have to go," she said abruptly.

"Wait," he said.

She glanced at him.

"You're upset about the sister."

"I'm not upset," she said.

She was upset. Before, they had been laughing.

"She'll get you in trouble."

"I'm going." She climbed on her bike and without saying more, she rode off.

He had failed at the friendship. And he had not learned to swim.

She left and he saw the yellow of Olive's sweater move through the spaces between the trees.

Samir stayed alone at the beach. He pulled his phone out. He took pictures of the river, the way it was drawing in, leaving almost no place for his feet on the sand.

They didn't have this in Worcester or Nepal. He sent the photo to Heera. She called him right away.

He said, "Do you remember when we went into the country that day from the camp and we bathed in the river?"

"Yes, we were little. I remember my feet on the stones as we walked to the water. Nothing like the beach where you are."

"It was shallow," he said.

"Is it deep there?"

"I think yes." He held the phone up so she could watch the moving water.

"Just between you and me, Bahini, when I feel the water, I fear that a current will take me away." He didn't say, like it happened for Hajurama. "I don't like it when I feel the water push me."

"I don't remember what the river felt like," she said.

"I was swimming with Olive."

"The wild girl?"

"She isn't afraid of the river."

"Hajurba is homesick," Heera said. "I see it in his eyes when we talk. The one thing that makes his eyes shine is telling us to swim in the river."

After the call, Samir stepped again to the river's edge. A mist fell over the water, and in the fuzzy outline of the landscape, he had a fantasy of waking in a new place. He held his grandmother in his mind in this new place which was at a different river's bank. She was a young mother with a single braid down her back. The story had it that when they fled from Bhutan, she slipped on a riverbank and fell into the fast-moving river in a heavy, heavy rain.

In Samir's fantasy, he dove into the water and swam beside her in the current. He swam imagining some of the movements of Olive's arms. Pushing out and your body twists. The stretch in his back he knew from dance. The other arm would almost grab the water as he pulled back.

He swam in this way for as long as he needed with his hajurama, so she was not alone when her soul passed to the other side.

27

OLIVE

Just when she crashed on the glider, a text came in from Mom.

"Would you take the irises I painted for Simone when you go? I can't get there tonight."

"Gabe's picking me up in the morning after he gets off work."

That was the plan. She'd throw stuff on the seat. Mount her bike on the back. Tonight he was fishing.

"It's her birthday."

Oh, shit, thought Olive. "Do I have to?"

"Yes."

"Okay."

"What's wrong?"

So much.

• • •

Olive climbed the steps to the screened entryway of the Boudreaus' house. She pictured Simone with a protest sign, *This Is Our Land.*

Olive knew what Simone saw at the cove. She had seen Olive laughing. She and Samir were running with the gulls like kids and his serious eyes were deep brown and smiling under his shaggy eyebrows.

The entryway was densely packed with stools made of tree trunks, hanging plants, wood for burning. Nero yelped with joy to see her.

Olive stepped up into the small kitchen. The floors were worn wood. Gabe's father had patched the house up over the years. Through the kitchen and tiny living room was a deck where some of the family gathered.

She hesitated. Kyle was in the living room and she didn't want to talk to him.

There was Gabe's little cousin, Lily, in a tulle skirt tied with a big ribbon. Past the deck, Olive saw Lily's mom with Julia in the garden.

Kyle was framed by the trailing ivies hanging behind him. He saw her. "You marry him yet?"

That's how he said hey.

"I just finished my junior year," Olive said. She went on in. She touched her cheek to the bristles on his face. She could barely see the blue that shone from slits where his eyes were.

"He needs to get in at the Yard," Kyle said. "Loved the Navy. I was loyal. And I was good. I tell Gabe, the Navy Yard will take care of you." He told Olive this each time they met.

"I was twenty years at the Yard, and they gave me thirty days when I got the boot. Thirty days. You know, because I cursed out a wetback, a cockroach." He slapped his calloused hand hard on the knot-holed pine table and she jumped.

He looked really sick, but he whispered, "You can't even tell the truth anymore. Not if you're white."

"I'm just going to go see Simone." She wished she hadn't come.

From the deck, Olive saw Simone racing circles on her small bike around the track, head down. She maneuvered every curve with the ease of a bird.

"Happy birthday, Simone," Olive called.

Julia and Lily's mom were watering the flowers. Soon their arms would be full of daisies and irises. Simone had dismounted and soon she banged up the deck stairs.

She didn't look at Olive but said, "We already sang Happy Birthday when Gabe was here. But go on, there's still plenty of pie."

Everything felt off in the house.

Simone glanced at her, just like she did when she saw Olive at the beach.

Olive held her gaze.

"I brought you some presents," she said. "Nine little ones to stretch out your birthday, and a present from Mom."

Simone looked even smaller now without the shoulder pads and helmet — gangly and fine-boned.

Simone gave Olive a slice of pie. Olive wanted to take the edge from Simone's eyes.

"You always want blueberry pie for your birthday."

Kyle snored.

They sat on the steps. Lily watched, and Olive handed Simone an origami boat she'd folded. And inside were nine little presents, including the iris picture.

"From Mom and me," Olive said. "You have to open up just one a day and your birthday will last longer. Some are tiny. Some are places we can go."

"Which one can I open now?"

"You can pick."

She chose the longest little package and ripped it open. Inside were nine-year-old-sized pink glamour sunglasses.

"I'm a star," she said, but she didn't put them on. Lily put them on and had to hold them with both hands.

"I was on TV at the rally." Simone's eyes lit up. "It's because of immigrants my father lost his job at the Yard."

Simone sprang down the steps, squinted back at Olive. Lily was in her footsteps.

"Yeah, I remember," Olive said. She watched her from the porch. It was hard to breathe.

"They fired him at the Yard," Simone said. "They can pay other people less than my dad. That's how I know. Immigrants got the jobs."

Olive waited.

"They're not American," she added.

Olive thought of Bhim, who loved his bike in America.

"He won't be with you long," Simone said. "That boy you swim with."

"I don't swim with him," she said. "I was teaching him."

"He's about to get locked up, deported."

Now Olive came down the steps.

"What for?"

Olive placed her hands on Simone's shoulders. She didn't want her to turn away. *Tell me.*

"Who knows what can happen when immigrants come," Simone yelled. "Don't you wonder why anybody'd come here and not bother to talk English right? Why come? That's what my brother says."

She ran toward her bike beside the track.

Olive ran, too, and knelt down so she could really look in Simone's eyes. Nero laid his jowly head on Olive's thigh. Olive felt tightness in her throat.

"Don't you even wonder where Gabe is?" Simone said.

"I know he's fishing. We already planned tomorrow."

Simone jumped on the bike, slammed the starter, gunned the motor. Lily clapped.

She sang out the song Gabe blasted from his bike. "We are the ones who will never be broken," so sweet and clear beside the *braaap braaap braaap* of the bike.

Simone went back to taking the curves, this time faster and sharper.

Kyle stood at the open sliding glass door.

He called, "She'd jump off the high bridge if her brother said jump. Like somebody rips her heart out every time he leaves."

That night at home was the first time Olive searched online about hate groups. She sat cross-legged on the bathroom floor with her phone. She wanted to know.

She remembered a conversation with Lise.

"His dad Kyle's kind of out there. Some kind of racist liberty party."

"What's wrong with liberty?" Olive had asked.

"I mean like the kind of liberty for yourself to do whatever you want. But not other people."

She found the liberty people who hated laws. And neo-Nazi people shouting *Invaders, Go Home.*

28

SAMIR

Samir, Baba, Uncle and Bishnu sat cross-legged on the bare restaurant floor surveying the rectangular space. Bishnu, who had once had a restaurant and now had a store, was full of ideas.

He said, "Let me tell you about our momos. We had five kinds of momos. Momo will make or break you, my friend."

Baba broke out the paint and he and Samir stirred two cans — one a cross between pearl white and the palest of pink, the other a vibrant coral.

"Vegetable momo," Bishnu sang out, grabbing a paintbrush. "Friend momo, mixed momo, chicken chili momo, paneer and spinach momo."

"You said friend momo," Samir said. "You meant fried."

"Why not a friend momo?"

"Saathi momo," Uncle said. "This can be our signature dish." Uncle had also had a restaurant. "In my restaurant —"

"It was a food truck," Baba said.

"Yes, and we went to food truck festivals all over New England, and you know who came?"

"Hungry people!"

"Momoliscious," he recalled. "I loved my truck."

Samir painted the slightly grand coral wall. It was a little bit of yellow, orange and pink. Heera had picked it, and he could imagine her laughing joyfully as the long side wall of the restaurant turned bright coral.

"I'll tell you who came to Momoliscious," Uncle said. "White people. People looked out for us during COVID. People bought online. Some were Peace Corps people. Two men came, they were trekkers. They lived in Nepal five years. A woman — she had been in the Peace Corps in a Tamang village. A lot of Peace Corps, that was who came. They will find you. You could call this restaurant Saathi Momo. They came for friendship."

Uncle painted the other long wall the very pale pink. Bishnu answered the door for delivery men who brought in many wooden chairs made of dark mahogany Baba had bought in bulk. They placed the chairs in a row down the middle of the room.

Later they stopped for a break and got takeout from Dragonfly China at the corner of the strip mall. They sat in a row on the mahogany chairs and ate takeout.

They argued, they leapt up and danced, they told stupid jokes.

"Once there was a shopkeeper and he had a business

model of pay now, pick up tomorrow. So everyday people came in to pay now. But when they came the next day to pick up, what they paid for had not arrived."

They men absolutely cracked up at this. "Pay now, pick up tomorrow!"

Stuffed with Chinese food, they went back to names for the restaurant.

"Delicacies from Shangri-La," Bishnu said and tried to nod solemnly. "Americans are very romantic about a secret place in the Himalayas where there are no problems."

They went back to painting, tossing out more names and rumbling with laughter.

They had always been like this since Samir could remember.

He FaceTimed Heera. He walked in a circle and scanned the walls with his phone for Heera to see.

"Oh," she sighed. "Sundara. I want to come. This is the beautiful color."

"Auntie is bringing plants," he said. "She said we must have a million paper lanterns and a wall of ivies and more plants and lots of flowers."

"I'll paint the walls with good-luck flowers," Heera told Samir. "For the day we open, I'll make a shrine above it with a huge prayer flag with wind horses. Beautiful block prints of horses."

Everyone shouted hello to Heera and she shouted hello back to them.

Baba said, "Let me see your mother."

He sat huddled on one of the chairs in the center, bent over Samir's phone. Maybe he was making sure she had eaten.

"Don't forget to stop studying and have a healthy plate of maam. Yes. You and Heera pick the colors," Samir heard him say. "When is your exam? Tell me again so we imagine the day is coming. We are preparing for you here. Yes, Lakshima. Bring the poster of Lakshima."

They talked about the Himalayan flags to hang, red, white, blue, yellow, green. And of course the pictures of the temples.

Samir taped the dark wood floor with strips of masking tape and began to paint the baseboards and trim a deep maroon. Bishnu and Uncle teased him about the River's Tale diner.

"Bring all the tricks of the trade, chora."

"Dishwasher boy," they teased.

Samir was okay to keep painting while the men gossiped and joked. His mind went to the River's Tale, where the workmen gossiped and joked. They were friends to each other.

Baba got off the phone. He told them all the items Ama and Heera were preparing and would bring. They had found a carpet runner that was also coral and woven with flowers. They found dark maroon fabric embossed with petals and were sewing covers for the cushions of the yellow couch where people would wait for a table when the restaurant was full. Heera said she'd wear marigolds in her hair.

Then Bishnu hauled in his portrait of the Seven Horses, which he said were auspicious for the birth of this new restaurant. They couldn't hang the pictures yet because the paint was wet. They set the picture propped up in a chair. And they ate with the seven white stallions racing through both clouds and water, bringing strength and success.

His mind went to Olive. They had laughed and chased around the beach, leaping over the fallen tree trunks and sea creatures and splashing the water.

A possible friend. Yes.

But he had failed. He painted and thought of his friends in Pathri when they lived in the same place and did things together. They watched videos that taught them dance moves. They helped each other with math. There was even a kid in Worcester who made a playlist for Samir.

Was there a gift he could make?

What could he do for Olive who was teaching him to swim? Something that would show he could be a friend? It could not be thought of as a payment.

There was something about her that was sad. He had seen her alone on her porch playing her guitar.

In the restaurant, he moved on to the baseboard beneath the coral wall where they would hang the shrine, swishing the brush with the maroon paint. He imagined the prayer flag with wind horses that Heera would hang on this wall. He remembered how Olive liked the horse he drew. When Olive saw the horse on the small island, this Lord of the Fishes seemed to bring her joy. She called to him. She drew a picture of him in the sand,

He wanted to do something that would bring her joy.

29

OLIVE

Olive rushed through the busy Saturday morning farmers market on an errand for her mother. Area farmers set up tents or the beds of their pickups in the parking lot down from the River's Tale and beside the CVS, the post office, Luna's Salon. The farmers brought vegetables, cut flowers wrapped in twine, honey, homemade balm for sunburn and bites, oatmeal bread and sweet buns warm from the oven. The loaves of bread were under tea towels in the back of a pickup and looked like a low mountain range.

Julia had a space beside the baker's pickup, but it was empty. She wasn't here yet.

Past them were chickens for sale. And every size of egg from a pullet to a duck egg.

Today children pressed into a petting zoo with white

baby goats chewing up the paper signs, lambs, crying piglets and a small black-eared donkey.

That's when she saw Samir racing beside Mr. Paudel, who was on his yellow bike. His knees circled round and round in loose-fitting cotton pants. Samir wore an apron, and he must have been on a quick break from the River's Tale, maybe to make sure his grandfather locked his bike.

But when he dismounted, he walked it, wearing his jacket with creases like veins in the leather part. Before them, a man spun cotton candy around a wooden stick. "Come on up. Come and get it. Cotton candy. Popcorn," the man called out in his carnival voice and held out a stick with the sugary pink air. But Mr. Paudel wanted the popcorn that came in small boxes.

Samir was in a hurry, and he called something in Nepali. Mr. Paudel peered into the spinner as the mound of cotton candy grew as big as his wide jaw, his cheekbones, his whole head with a purple knitted cap pulled over his ears.

But it was a box of popcorn he picked up.

The sign read $3. Samir pulled out three ones from his pocket and paid. Mr. Paudel gobbled mouthfuls of popcorn.

Samir walked the bike.

"In just a second, Ethel will come to find you," Olive said, catching up to them. Mr. Paudel brought his hands together while holding the popcorn.

"He wants to see the goats," Samir said. "They make him think of home and my grandmother."

Olive remembered the grandfather went to the cove to sing to her spirit.

"They make me think of a story," his grandfather said.

Mr. Paudel stuffed more popcorn in his mouth. "I will tell you a story." He offered popcorn to Samir.

"I don't have time. Not now," Samir said.

Ahead in a pen, the young goats banged their horn nubs into each other, calling out their goat songs and ringing their bells.

Mr. Paudel lifted his arms and popcorn in the air, swayed his hips, turned in slow circles.

Samir turned away.

"He says he's become a young man in his mind. So he's singing an old village song like he sang to my grandmother, like girls and boys took turns singing lines to each other. He sings that he will come across to her on the other side and eat her popped corn."

He shrugged, glancing at Olive.

"They were farmers."

It was late morning under a seamless blue sky. Some strangers smiled at Mr. Paudel's joy, and a little girl passing by lifted her arms to dance with him.

"Hey, Paudel, break's over." Ethel was at the railing of the River's Tale deck in her tights and mini skirt. "Last I knew you're on the clock."

She was short, unsmiling. She ruled everyone by simply raising her eyebrows.

Samir leaped up the steps.

"Take the bike inside when you get home," Samir called. Mr. Paudel was on his way, pedaling, the bike swaying, zigzagging side to side.

Olive looked behind her. Samir was stacking plates and watched by the picnic tables on the River's Tale deck.

Something was uneasy in the way he paused and held his body still as Mr. Paudel disappeared up the hill of Chestnut Street.

Olive turned down the rows of vendors to the baker's stand to buy a loaf of bread from his mountain range of loaves. She picked a loaf. It was still warm.

Then she heard a shout, very loud. A kid she vaguely knew from school was running from the Day Night back to the café.

"That man!" he shouted. "That man."

He shouted to Samir who was balancing a tray of dirty plates on the deck.

The smell of cooking meat carried on the wind from the Greek vendor's cart in the market along with the sweet smell of the animals' hay.

What man?

Samir ran past the tent and the hardware store. Olive saw his T-shirt in the distance disappear around a truck at the pump.

People were paused with hands reaching for a loaf of bread or a pot of nasturtiums, searching for why there was shouting.

Olive put down the bread and ran out of the market, too, and followed the direction Samir took, cutting through parking lots and between kids on scooters.

She ran after Samir and the other boy, panting, climbing Chestnut Street where it rose above the market.

"There!" the boy shouted.

Beneath a low limb of a tree, Olive saw a splash of yellow. Samir let out a high-pitched cry that sounded not like a boy, more like the whine of a gull.

Olive ran.

People were talking. *Like those kids who come on J-1 visas for summer jobs. They come here. They don't wear helmets. I've seen 'em ride in the rain under a bag. They can't even see where they're going.*

She ran, feeling a wave of nausea.

Samir was on his knees in a circle of people.

Mr. Paudel was on the ground.

An accident. I don't know. From where I was, all I saw was a pickup with a green stripe go by and then this guy was over in the bushes like that.

Mr. Paudel's leg, spine and arm were slightly bent like fallen branches. Samir lurched toward him and placed his arms around his grandfather's small body.

Samir was talking but Olive couldn't understand the words.

Samir didn't know what to do. He didn't know people were standing around him. He put his hands beneath his grandfather's head in the purple cap.

Olive got out her phone and called 911.

The voice said, "Is he breathing?"

Since Chris died, she'd taken the lifesaving class where she learned CPR, though she knew with fentanyl you start CPR, then the Narcan, too.

Now she called him, "Hajurba, Hajurba." He didn't open his eyes.

She brought her ear beside his mouth to feel his breath. She knew this. Too late for Chris. She knew now.

If she didn't feel his breath she knew where to place the

heel of her hand, find that bone between his nipples, place her other palm on top. Press.

Tears fell down her face.

She became very still and waited for the feel of his breath.

"Is he breathing?" the voice spoke from the phone.

She felt the slightest touch of air on her cheek.

"Yes," she said.

"The EMTs are almost there."

"Yes."

Ms. Geeta was there. Olive was aware of the flash of colors of her sari.

Olive heard the sound of an ambulance siren. Ms. Geeta and Samir seemed to want to lift him up and carry him home.

Olive said, "A doctor's coming."

Mr. Paudel had not moved.

Ms. Geeta knelt and gently folded up the edges of his cap. The cap was dark with wetness. Olive saw Samir's hand was dark red and it was his grandfather's blood.

So fast. A guy, blue shirt, beside them. Stethoscope. Bitter coffee on his breath. And he was pressing gauze to the side of Mr. Paudel's head. He kept adding more gauze and never lifted the pressure of his hands on the side of Mr. Paudel's head.

Samir did not seem to notice who was with them. He spoke softly by his grandfather's ear. His own body pressed against his grandfather's jacket.

Olive pulled away. She still felt the breath on her cheek.

"Hey, buddy," the EMT said. "Can you open your eyes? Hey, bud. This your boy here? Talk to me."

"He's my grandfather," Samir said.

"Your granddad — he speak English?" the EMT asked.
"Not much."

"Tell him he needs to show us he can open his eyes."

A police car sped in. Olive heard the ring of the tires across the bridge deck at the creek near the River's Tale.

What if Hajurba had been hit there? He could have been swept into the river. She knew Samir couldn't swim, but he'd have gone in after his grandfather.

Olive became aware of the talk around her. The officer was asking bystanders, "What happened here? What did you see?"

Suddenly, Olive was aware of a T-shirt she knew. The face that was tanned and freckled. The sandy hair.

Gabe was in the circle, too.

"Could have been a hit and run. Or could have been the driver didn't know what happened. I mean, the dude was on the wrong side of the road."

"Wasn't a hit and run." Gabe's voice.

Olive squinted at him in the sun. She began to shake.

"I passed the guy. I didn't know he fell."

The officer said, "You the driver in the pickup?"

"I was in a pickup. I kept my distance from him. I know the law," Gabe said.

"But you saw the victim? What happened?"

"The guy was swerving. I swear it looked like …"

Olive stared at him.

"Gabe!" she called over all the voices in the crowd.

He didn't look at her. "Gabe!"

Their voices faded as the officer and Gabe moved away from the circle.

She couldn't follow because now the cop with the Paudels was questioning her. "Miss, are you related?"

She shook her head.

He wanted her information. She gave it.

What did she see? She told him.

Gabe was beside her.

"It's okay," he said. "I'll talk to the cops. You're okay."

She looked at him, confused. What was he saying? Was he saying he was in the truck?

She wasn't okay. No one was okay.

He was gone. He wore the owl T-shirt she gave him.

Other cops shot photos of the bike, the scene. When the officer came to talk to Samir, Olive couldn't see a trace of Gabe. He had not talked to any of the Paudels. He talked to the cops.

"How old is he?"

"Sixty-seven," Samir said like a stone. He shook so badly he could hardly speak.

An image of Gabe's hand shoving Samir toward the waves flashed in front of Olive just as the ambulance engine revved. Light glinted on the yellow bike.

"Go home. They won't take a minor in the ambulance. You coming?" he said to Ms. Geeta, but she didn't under-stand or was too shaken. Olive knew she wouldn't go and leave Bhim, who must be waiting at home.

The medic gave Ms. Geeta a card. On it he wrote the name of the hospital where they were taking Mr. Paudel. *Mersea Medical*, it read. *Award-Winning Community Care*.

The ambulance put on its flashers and alarms. It sped past the orange and red Day Night sign.

Ms. Geeta began to run to their house and to Bhim. Gabe was gone.

It was just Olive and Samir with the bike. Samir was still shaking. His knees nearly gave way as they climbed the street. The tires jammed. They lifted the bike.

She wondered if his mother and Heera would come. His father would have to come from work. How would they get from one place to another? A car was rarely in their driveway. People worked long hours.

Was Samir in charge? He couldn't talk.

They arrived at their houses. The old SUV was in Samir's dirt driveway.

It was close to the time Gabe had been going to come to the house to pick her up. They had planned he'd come when he got off work.

All she could see was Mr. Paudel's silent face. And the truck.

She knew the truck with a green stripe. It was Kyle's.

She and Samir were inside his gate. The sprawling lilac tree protected them from the street.

"He'll be okay," Olive said. His eyes flashed to hers. "I mean, there'll be a doctor in the emergency room. They're taking him to a doctor."

Samir dropped his head into his hands. She was so close she felt his body shake, his legs, his ribs. She placed her hand on his back to stop the shaking. He closed his eyes against the light.

Then he touched her shoulders and brought her face to his chest.

She let his body shake against hers.

Loud voices came from the open windows of his house.

She said, "We'll take my mother's car. We'll go to the hospital."

But he turned and vanished into the world she had no entry to.

30

SAMIR

Baba had already arrived and was speaking on the phone. He motioned to Samir to get in the car. Samir's aunt talked loudly to Uncle and Bhim. She described the medic and Hajurba's head that was bleeding and about all the people.

In a second, Samir's phone would ring.

His phone rang.

"Is Hajurba talking?" Heera's voice was high-pitched.

"No. He was not conscious. He was bleeding. They stopped the bleeding."

Only silence on the phone.

"He was breathing." Samir's voice was a monotone. "We're going to the hospital. I'll call you."

"You should have come back to Worcester." Heera was crying. "What does a restaurant matter?"

They had talked about it all. Their family had carefully made the choices.

This prosperous city by the sea.

A chance of a lifetime.

A restaurant in a city with tourists and money.

Ama's sanitation certificate. The restaurant certificate.

Baba, the businessman.

If you want to wake up, come to Nepal.

"Ama and I are driving there now," Heera said. And then, "What is the matter with this country?"

"I'll call," he said again.

Samir and Baba climbed into their old van. It was a clear, breezy Saturday. Samir was with his father who did not show his feelings. But Samir could see his father's lips. They were quivering, and Baba had to bring his hands to his lips to try to steady himself so that he could drive.

They did not talk because they were so full of fears they couldn't say.

In the emergency room, the hours stacked on each other like bricks.

Finally, a person called Baba in, and Samir watched his father pass through the secured doors of the ER, and then he couldn't see his father anymore. They only let Baba in.

Samir waited. He called Heera. He talked with her in a hushed voice.

"What happened?" she said.

"I don't know."

"Did you see ..."

"I saw nothing. He was alone."

But then he remembered the police asking questions. He

remembered Olive bent to Hajurba's mouth, listening. Her hands on his chest, the bloody jacket.

He remembered her talking to the EMT. He remembered Gabe's voice.

But no boy would hurt a grandfather.

All he could do was breathe and hope the breath helped his family. He tried to imagine that much hate a boy could have.

Hours later Baba came out.

"They have put stitches where his head is cut. He is not awake. They have done many tests. Now they are putting him in a room."

Baba looked drawn and very, very sad. Samir and his father found their way to the floor where Hajurba had been taken.

In the room, Samir found his grandfather with a large white bandage around his head, with an IV dripping into a needle in his arm.

"They want to watch him for concussion," Baba said.

On the phone, Samir could hear Auntie saying, "Tell them you want to bring him home. We can watch him. He needs to eat. Bring him home."

The hospital room was cold and silent, with just the sound of a machine on the second person's side that was like his external breath. It hummed in and out. It chilled them all.

They waited — standing or praying cross-legged on the floor beside Hajurba who did not open his eyes. People came in and out. They took blood. They measured the beat of his heart. They rolled him away to do something called a CAT scan. Sun set and then it was dark in the room.

Baba decided to go home and get food. He would bring food for his son and his father.

Samir found Hajurba's jacket in the hospital closet. He wiped blood off the leather collar and epaulets in the sink, dried the jacket off and put it on.

His thoughts went in many directions.

Maybe he and Baba should take Hajurba back to Pathri. He remembered the sound of crickets in the night in New Hampshire. They came from a wet place in the woods behind their house. He wished he did not know that sound. He remembered the silence of a branch falling into the snow in the early morning behind the River's Tale.

His life in America had been chipotle aioli burgers, spicy dip and fries in addition to dal bhat. Here there were dogs people loved better than cows. He knew the hum of the cities where he had lived. He had not seen toilet paper in Pathri.

Can you go back to where you started?

He watched his grandfather breathe.

But how can they stay in a place where a person is hated? He thought of the river. The river could kill you but it didn't hate you. That kind of killer he wanted to face. Even if he hated the pressure of the water on his body. He would do it without the girl. He would do it because he knew it would give his grandfather more peace in his mind if his grandchildren learned to swim in the river in this country.

If Samir did that, Hajurba would call the family in Nepal and tell them, like he did when Samir made the honor roll. He would say, Samir has swum across the river.

But what if Samir had never come here? What if he were

what his grandfather once was, a farmer growing cardamom on the mountainside? What if his mother sang while she spread the rice to dry? And Hajurama was still alive? What if he never saw the bird of New Hampshire or the silence of a branch falling in snow? What if he didn't have to learn to swim?

He lay down in the jacket on the floor beside Hajurba's bed so he would hear when his grandfather woke up.

"He is sleeping," he texted Heera.

"Baba will bring me as soon as we come."

When Baba came with food, he and Samir ate silently. They stayed with Hajurba together.

Samir added another vital reason to train in the water. He would build his muscular midsection and back — the muscles a boy needs to fight.

31

OLIVE

Olive's mother wasn't in the art room. She wasn't wearing the ragged blue shirt that made her eyes look like the sea. It had been Olive's.

Did all families wear each other's clothes? Maybe she'd gone for groceries. Olive watched the street.

She noticed the details of the room in a new way, as if everything could be a clue. The picture on the wall had been there all Olive's life. The bag-of-bones horse and the skinny knight.

Olive dropped to the floor beside the picture. Mr. Paudel's blood had dried on her fingertips and when she touched it, it was flaky.

Was it from Samir's shirt?

She had to find out what happened. How could you find

out the truth when people you loved only told you some things? Or you didn't know if they did or did not? Olive remembered the security camera that Officer Byatt wanted the Paudels to mount on their back wall. They could see who might be coming or going, people who could slip from the trail behind the scrubby woods between the houses and the street. There were lots of ways to get in.

Would that be the same person who passed Mr. Paudel on the street so close he fell, or they ran the side of their truck with a stripe into Mr. Paudel's yellow bumper? Was someone working at the site today? What vehicle did they have?

She wanted to see for herself.

It was one o'clock. Gabe hadn't come or texted. Did that mean he was innocent but the police were still asking him questions? Or did it mean he could have tried to hurt Mr. Paudel?

She opened the front door and found her brother on the steps.

Chris! This time he surprised her.

Hey. He had grown a beard, and his eyes looked blood-shot and worn.

I was going, she said.

I'll come. Even though he looked like he needed to crash.

Chris clambered down the porch stairs beside her, yawning. She put her hand on his shoulder.

He was bigger than Gabe, broader with bigger bones. She had forgotten.

Where we going?

To the new Creek development, she said. *There was an*

accident. The grandfather. He got hit and got thrown from his bike.

She had a flash of the image of Mr. Paudel's legs on the ground, bent at the knee like he was running. He'd struck his head. The EMTs kept his body very supported when they lifted him in case anything else was hurt.

Kyle worked on a house on a street that was beyond the winding streets of brick row houses. Bhim had told Olive in great detail.

Olive ran down a fork of one path and another until she came to a street where the houses changed from shabby brick to split entry. Chris stayed by her side.

Coming through a stand of pines, she saw Kyle up a ladder nailing boards to the lathe. He worked, wheezing and coughing. Out in the street was the Prius. Behind it was a trailer loaded with boards. Not hooked up to the car.

Can a Prius haul construction stuff?

Sure, Chris said. *We used it to haul dirt bikes.*

Kyle was driving and they made a switch. Or Gabe was driving.

Chris smelled like smoke.

Got me, he finally said. He was inside her head. *Whatever happened, I know the son's not the same as the father.*

So Gabe might not have?

Talk to him. Chris meant Gabe.

Gabe didn't call and she didn't call him. Last thing he said was he was talking to the cops. He said they were okay. They had both let the time go by, the time they had set.

Mom brought home nasturtiums and was digging in the garden. No one across the street was home.

She didn't text Gabe. She thought something would become clearer. There would be some official explanation.

Olive paced the porch. By evening, cars lined the street. She watched for Heera. Olive went to Samir's Instagram where she found a link to Heera on TikTok. She was dressed in blue. She danced, lifting her arms and miming the words of a song in Nepali. She wore glasses with large round frames.

Olive came inside, closed the front door.

What if Gabe wasn't driving the truck? What if it was Kyle? Gabe would take the hit.

The son is not the same as the father.

Olive texted him.

He texted straight back.

"The cemetery."

If there was just some way she could have her life the way it had been.

It was 8 p.m. when they both got there. The air was warm and humid.

By the back gate, Olive found the two-tone truck with the green streak along its body, not the Prius. When she opened the passenger door, Nero was stretched out along the small back seat.

She climbed in beside Gabe.

He didn't talk. She could see his eyes and then he grabbed her and held her body to his.

It had been three days since they had been together. Their breath steamed up the windows in the humid air.

"I helped him breathe," she whispered. "I didn't under-stand how he could be so hurt. What happened?"

"Just let me hold you a second." He put his lips into her hair, then brought his warm mouth over hers.

"Tell me," she said.

She shut her eyes and for a second it was natural and safe for their bodies to protect each other.

His voice was husky.

"The guy was almost in the middle of the road, wobbling. Like he was drunk. What the Christ was he doing there?"

Then Gabe let out a wail and the truck shook. It was as if Chris had just died and he was crying the same unbelieving grief. Nero inched forward until he lowered his head on Gabe's shoulder.

"You were in your dad's truck?" she said. "This truck."

"I felt this rage," Gabe continued in that unnatural voice. He opened his window all the way down to give them enough air to breathe. "But I was three feet away. I stayed three feet away. The law says three feet. I knew I could make it past him. And just then the old man zigzags."

She was trying to hold Gabe's words straight in her mind.

"The street opened out a hundred yards before the Day Night," Gabe said.

Olive knew that opening of the road. She imagined she and Gabe were there in the truck on the street where she'd lived all her life.

The dog lay back down. He shuddered an exhale.

She loved them both. They were her life.

Olive imagined them coming to the slight opening of the road that morning. Hajurba was pumping hard to get up the hill on Gabe's right. She felt Gabe's hands grip the steering wheel with rage.

In the truck now, the smell of dog and sweat closed in around her.

"They're none of our business." Gabe's shoulders shook, which made the car window rattle in its casing. It took Olive a while to understand that his body was shaking against the door.

"But what happened?"

"Somehow the old man lost control. It happened so fast. I didn't hit him. Three feet. That's what I told the cops when I heard he went over. I wasn't for sure he fell. The guy was in the middle of the goddamn road."

She also pictured that when the truck came alongside the bike, no one pulled over. Hajurba couldn't, and Gabe did the law.

"He was unconscious when they took him." And then she stopped because that nausea was rising in her again. "I'm going to the hospital. If you're not family they won't tell you anything." She spoke softly. "They won't tell you anything on the phone. Come with me."

"Listen to me." His voice dropped low. He whispered into her neck. "That kid's got nothing to do with me. And nothing to do with you."

She could feel his breath where she'd felt Mr. Paudel's breath. "Mr. Paudel does have to do with us."

"Like here we are in this country," he said. "Every man for himself. We're totally alone."

Everything they talked about came back to Chris.

"There was blood on me," Olive said. "It took a while to

stop the bleeding from his head."

"No country. No neighbors looking out for you. Just shame. And you got nothing to hold on to. All you got is shame for what you can't stop doing which is living your life with a loser's job. People like my father."

They were silent.

"Gabe," she said. "I heard about your dad. He's sick."

Gabe pulled away from her. "We can manage."

She could taste the tension in Gabe's house with his dad there.

"I wondered if your dad was the one driving the truck. This morning."

She could feel his spine stiffen. Gabe shoved open the truck door, left the door open, then went off somewhere in the dark like she'd heard dogs do when they're wounded.

Olive got out, too. The sky was gray and darkening. She waited.

When he didn't come, she called out, "I'm going, Gabe."

She switched on the little light Chris had fixed the bike up with and it still worked.

"Good night, Gabe," she called.

This was the day they were going to move in together, beginning with the weekend.

She headed down the center cemetery road. The truck's headlights shot on. Gabe pulled up and got out of the truck.

They didn't talk. She dismounted and he loaded her bike into the bed. Nero still slept in the back, sprawled like an elk. Gabe opened the passenger door for Olive. She got back in. He leaned in and put his head in her lap and held her thighs with his open hands.

"Oh my God I love you," he said like it was all one word.

She put her hands in his hair.

"I don't know what to do," she whispered.

32

SAMIR

It was morning, but no lights were on in Hajurba's room. The man in the first bed was asleep. Hajurba was in the second bed that overlooked a roof vent. Samir heard music from the other man's TV that sounded like the ocean. He wanted to smash the TV.

Samir lay on the floor by Hajurba's bed where he spent the night without sleep. He heard everything around him.

Now he heard the sound of the door.

When he saw Olive in the doorway, he jumped up like a rabbit.

"Can I come in?" she said.

He lifted his eyes briefly to hers, then looked past her. At first he wanted to stand between Olive and his grandfather, who looked as small as a boy in the bed. His head was still wrapped in a bandage and there were tubes running from his arm to a dripping bottle.

"How is he?" she said.

Samir calmly walked her back to the door and out of the room. He left her standing in the hall and shut the door. He would be polite. But she could not come in.

He heard a knock on the door again.

"I'm alone," she said, opening the door. She came farther in, passing the first patient, and stood by the curtain between the beds.

"It's hot in here," she said. She took off her sweater and wadded it into a ball.

He also hated the stagnant air of the place. Yesterday his grandfather had been singing a love song in the outdoor market.

A hissing sound came from small tubes pushing air into Hajurba's nose. A person had added this in the night.

"Why are you here?" Samir said.

He knew his eyes were bloodshot. His head was thick with no sleep. Without sleep, his mind was muddy. The hospital was full of beeps and lights and the roommate crying out. Machines tracked his grandfather's heart.

Olive waited. He did not want her here. She was not family. But he paused before he tried to walk her out of this room again.

She said, "I wanted to know if he's okay. No one answered at your house."

"He's sleeping." For a second, who she was didn't matter so much. Lack of his own sleep shut down some of Samir's anxiety.

What would Heera say?

She came. You could talk to her.

He stayed between his grandfather and Olive. "If I tell them Gabe Boudreau is harassing us, my father's friend says they will call us troublemakers. They will say we don't belong. Auntie says we should bring my grandfather home."

Samir turned away. He thought this was too much truth and Olive would walk out, so he waited for this to happen.

"They know the truck," Olive said. "Everybody saw the truck."

"My grandfather fell from the bike and hit the concrete curb," he said. "They put stitches in his head. Now he still sleeps. We don't know why he fell."

Olive sat down cross-legged on the floor and leaned her back against the wall between the hospital machines.

After a while she said, "Have you been here all night?"

"All night all day. People keep talking to me." He felt his face get tight with rage.

They both watched his grandfather breathe. Eventually, he accepted the sound of Olive's breathing, too.

Samir said, "I don't know if he is unconscious or just tired of everything. My family says bring him home. My aunt will take care of him. They are afraid."

Olive said, "I was afraid for my brother. We didn't have insurance to get him in a treatment center."

He glanced at her and took that in. Samir felt like he, too, knew his family had taken jobs just for the insurance. They had a little for Hajurba from the Affordable Care Act.

He said, "In the camp we didn't need insurance. Now it depends on the restaurant. My grandfather would be okay in the camp with the elders. In the camp they sang the old songs and lived in their memories, the old people. Because of me, Hajurba said, our future is America. Hajurba kept a clipping of the prince of Bhutan holding a soccer ball at his American school. He laughed and said, 'And now my grandson can go to school in America, too.'"

A nurse came in. With her fingers, she flicked the tube that connected the liquid in the bottle to Hajurba's arm. The bottle was nearly empty.

"Sleep will help him," she said. "Sleep," she repeated and brought her palms together and placed her cheek to the back of her hand.

"I speak English," Samir said. "Can he go home today?"

"Let's let him wake up," she said.

When the nurse was gone, Olive asked, "Are you supposed to be at work?"

"Yes." He had just remembered.

"I know Ethel. She has no mercy. Did you call in?"

He had not. Right then, he texted Ethel's cell. She did not respond. In a few minutes he texted again.

"If you want, I'll tell her what happened. See if she'll grant you a reprieve."

Samir thought of all the goodbyes in the camp. They were always having to say goodbye, never knowing for how long. "I ♥ u" and "miss u," they texted. Samir wore a rubber wristband, kept the bracelet Heera gave to him on Bhai Tika in his pocket.

He turned the rubber bracelet inside out. He inked a few

words he still knew how to write in Nepali besides his name: *I love you*. He held it up to dry. He slid the wristband on Hajurba's wrist with his hospital tag — *Paudel, Mahendra* and the day that he was born.

He dreamed blood revenge.

He would never hurt Samir's family again.

33

OLIVE

Olive went to the River's Tale early the next morning before work. It was a little after seven.

She looked up at the back deck of the River's Tale. She knew she'd have to schmooze a while, because what a person could get from Ethel depended on relationship and loyalty.

Today an American flag hung at half-mast from the deck. It was about a soldier. Ethel knew when any local boys in the New Hampshire Guard were deployed. And when one was lost, she knew.

Today the "Soldiers" song pumped out over the deck — the same song Simone sang. *"It's time to strap our boots on/ This is the perfect day to die."*

The familiar music wrapped around Olive, and she climbed the steps of the café.

She sat at the counter, letting herself feel a little safety in the music and familiar talk. People ordered crullers and eggs over easy and she watched Ethel's stern lips crack into a smile when she told a story about her little girl, Isobel — how she sold mud pies from her own make-believe café. Ethel wore her hair curly today and tied up in a green headband.

Olive asked for a coffee, and Ethel also brought her a cruller still warm.

"How you doing, you and your mom? How's Gabe? I see him around with that hound in the back of his car. He makes me smile, the way he loves that dog."

Had she seen them up the street on Saturday morning?

"Yeah, we're good," Olive said.

She was about to tell her about Samir still being at the hospital when Ethel scrolled to a photo of a little brunette with a bow in her hair, an apron around her three-year-old self and her hands on her hips.

Two empty booths filled up with workmen who came wiping sweat from their eyes.

"Ethel …" Olive began.

"Got to get them," Ethel said. "Say hey to your mom."

Olive heard her talking to the men.

"Yeah, short-staffed. The kid never showed up." She stood with her hands on her hips like her little girl. "I mean, this place opens at six in a blizzard. And he never showed up on a perfectly good day."

"That the kid you got washing dishes? What is he, Mexican? His father or grandfather or somebody in that family got in a bike accident. Pretty bad. Right out here in the road."

"Yeah, right. He left me in the lurch. Forget it with him. I'm not hiring that kind anymore. Customers weren't that crazy about him."

Olive stood up. "He's at the hospital, Ethel," she shouted. "I came to tell you he's still with his grandfather. You must have heard about the bike accident. His grandfather got knocked unconscious in the road. You can't fire him for that."

Ethel stared at her wide-eyed. Nobody talked back to Ethel.

"He did call and he texted. And nobody picked up."

"That's 'cause I was doing all of my job and all of his. He's not my cup a tea, that kid."

"How many people have to get hurt before somebody thinks something's wrong?" Olive, who was wearing her red bathing-suit top and jeans, reached her bare arms out to them, but nobody answered. So she shouted, "He's a dancer. Have you ever seen how perfect he dances?"

A line was forming at the register, and Ethel turned away, shaking her head. "Jesus Christ, you'd think the heat wave was making people crazy. Chill out, my girl."

Olive put some cash by the cup of coffee on her way out. What good did it do Samir for her to scream at Ethel?

At 8 a.m., children and counselors were gathering in the main hall.

Gabe texted. "Can I see you?"

A dozen children swarmed at each table with food in the middle for counselors to pass around. Mr. Farley talked to the kids about today's nature treasure hunt.

"If you look under the moss on fallen bark, you will find a world of life beneath. See how many insects you can find on bark."

After breakfast, the children found tons of bugs and squiggled them in their nature notebooks. They also heard the wood wren and went chasing after its song. They raced to the shore and found crabs under the stones and decided these could count as very large bugs. They watched a lobsterman heading out the creek.

Then they were all on their hands and knees searching for what was on the forest floor or in the sand among the rocks. Natalie screamed when she found a very dead, dried-up crab.

Olive turned her phone off. She was too busy with the kids and dead crabs. She kept seeing the old man riding his yellow bike dressed like a Navy pilot. Buttercups like a blanket across their weedy grass. Samir dancing in the woods like nothing could touch him.

Then they had snacks — hand pies with blueberries and cartons of milk. Followed by ten things to explode your mind about bugs.

Everything looked shockingly bright green and blue at the camp. Olive took it all in as she kept the children out of the water and on task.

When camp ended, Olive got out her phone. She searched *Pathri*, the name of the camp where Samir had friends. What came up was a Pathri in a district in India. But he hadn't said India.

Pathri Nepal camp. A video came up of dust roads and small huts. They just looked like slats of wood. The camera rose high over a city of hut after hut, one next to the other underneath a canopy of leaves.

She imagined Mr. Paudel telling stories in this place, sitting under one of the trees. And one of his stories was about a horse.

She would go to the cove and take a photo of the horse that he drew from his English class. And get it to him in the hospital.

Can I see you? The text still lit her phone like a fire.

34

SAMIR

The beach at the cove was an empty space. Every time Samir had come, he was with only Hajurba or Olive. He did not know if Gabe came again after the first time they met here. It was a lonely stretch of beach. The trees were spindly. The tide ran up to their roots and submerged them two times a day.

Maybe that is why trees fell across the sand. It seemed eerie to him but it had become familiar.

When he arrived this afternoon, he heard Olive's voice. She was speaking loudly as if she were trying to throw her voice across the cove to the island. She held her hands wide to the spotted horse who shook his head. She was telling the horse he wasn't like any other horse and he was wild and splendid.

Then Olive grabbed her phone and snapped his picture.

The horse watched her, whinnied, then lowered his pale head to the field grass.

Samir whistled to the horse, and Olive spun around.

She watched him, unsure. He was taking off his shirt under the squirrely apple tree.

"I made that sound so I wouldn't scare you. I'm going to swim."

"I was talking to the horse. I thought I was alone."

"I thought I would be alone, too," he said.

"What were you going to do?"

"I am doing it. I am teaching myself to swim."

"You were going to swim alone here?"

"Yes. I will swim today."

"That's stupid to do it alone."

"That's what my sister said."

"How is your grandfather?"

"He's awake. He's eating now," Samir said.

"Your grandpa's a rock star."

Samir shrugged. He had put on his swim shorts with parrots on them that Hajurba made him buy. The first time he wore his jeans.

"You have trunks," Olive noted.

"I'm prepared," he said.

"I'll hang out a while so you don't die."

"I've planned a gift for you," he said.

"What?" she said.

"You have to wait."

"You can't just swim," she said.

"Soon," he said. "You'll think the gift is very good."

"You think we're swimming. To where? To the island?"

Her eyes were suspicious.

"If I swim," he called from the base of the tree. "My grandfather can feel more peaceful. The river took his wife. He thinks the river has power. Hajurba always said if he could swim, he would have saved our grandmother."

Olive stepped toward the surf and felt the rush of the water. She turned to the island.

"So you'll be the one who swims?" she said.

"And you will be the one who finds something good, too."

Samir thought she looked like lightning struck someplace inside her, and he felt proud to see that on her face.

They went to the rim of the beach — all that remained of it with the rising tide.

"Try this." Olive showed him how to stand, then squat. "Just enough to bring your head underwater."

She waded out, squatted down and popped up.

"Okay, then," Olive said. "Inhale when you stand, and exhale and blow bubbles out through your nose when you squat and your head is under water."

She showed him. Underwater, she made rolling cascades of bubbles.

He rose up and down blowing bubbles.

He stood. "I am not swimming. I'm ready to swim now."

"First, prepare," she said. "You have to show your body how to trust the water." She showed him floating on your belly. She stretched her body out on the river so that her heels, butt and head poked out.

He said, "I don't want to float. I will swim."

"When you float, you feel your buoyancy in the water

and you see how you can keep your body on the surface. You feel your own safety."

He had a moment of doubt. Should he trust her? What if she was someone that he could not trust after all? And now he would drown.

"But never alone. Heera is right," she said. "Stretch out. Hold your breath to the count of three. I'll leave my hand underneath you. You can float."

They went back to stand up, breathe in, squat down, breathe out bubbles. Then he stretched out on his belly — one, two, three — feet down. He did float on his belly. Then back on his feet. Olive's arms just touched him.

"After you feel fine about all these things, then we'll swim."

"No, show me ..." He stretched out on his belly. "Since we're both here, show me how to move."

She kept her arms beneath his belly. "Bring your hands to touch in front of you. Now kick. Try to keep your legs straight. You feel it in your hips. Ready? Arms in front. Take a breath. I'm with you. Face in the water. Now kick."

He kicked and he felt for the first time how he could propel himself on the surface. Not far. But he felt it.

"Now rest," she said.

They were in shallow water. He squatted. Put his head in the water. Allowed his legs to feel the buoyancy of the water and feel his legs lift. Then kicked and he moved himself a few feet, then a few yards. Olive was laughing and swimming to keep beside him.

"When you want to stop, lift your head. Feet down. See how you keep yourself on the surface. So you won't need to touch down. You'll feel safe even if the water is deep."

He almost did.

He planted both feet on the rocky bottom. He let a smile spread over his face. He exhaled deeply, letting some of his fear slide away.

"For a minute, it was simple," he said. "When you count, you give it rhythm."

"Yes," she said.

But they kept on practicing until he could float very well on both his stomach and his back and kick and move himself along the top. He could look into the sky as Olive had. He saw seagulls. Even better, he could blow bubbles and keep from breathing in the water.

He licked his lips. "It tastes like salt. Amazing. Like no river in Nepal. There was a river by the camp where Ama washed her hair and Heera and I played. It was warm. That was normal to me."

He propelled himself back out, then feet down.

"Show me one thing!"

"Yes."

"Your arms when you swim. Show me." He moved his own arms.

"First you have to breathe."

On her belly she showed him, turn your head to the right, take a breath, back to the water, turn your head to the left, take a breath, back to the water.

Over and over she did this.

"Now I want to do the arms."

"You're nothing like you were the first time," she said.

"No, I am nothing like that boy."

"Now watch how I turn my head to breathe when I lift my arm."

"I will watch," he said. He was shaking — not from the cold of the water, but at what he was about to do.

She swam out a ways, then turned toward him and swam her beautiful freestyle. It had a rhythm like a dance. Where he stood, he lifted his arms and followed her movements, and it was just like the memory he was already holding of her movements in his muscles.

"Use your back muscles," she said.

He felt his back lengthen and twist.

"That's the next lesson," she said.

"The arms, the breath, the kick."

"Yes."

On the shore Samir shivered. He looked out at the water, the island. For the flash of a second, fear filled him. Could he really do this? No one in his family had. He felt his skinny midsection. It was not any more muscular. But he could imagine his body swimming.

"Can your grandfather come home?" Olive asked.

He exhaled. "Yes, soon."

"Show him this." She grabbed her phone from her jeans pocket and scrolled through the pictures she'd taken. The horse was small but clear. He'd be able to see the dignity of the horse. Samir felt her excitement.

Olive sent the pictures to Samir's phone. "Tell him they're from me, okay?"

"Yes," he said. "You know this hospital? You know how to find the rooms."

"If you had a dirt-biker brother, you'd know the hospital.

231

You'd know every floor and where to get free snacks in the Intensive Care waiting room. Chris had broken collarbones, crushed lungs, broken fingers, dislocated shoulders. Mostly I know the ER. But it was easy to find your grandfather."

Samir said, "I am trying to be a friend. Am I doing it right? Are we friends now?"

She leaned down to grab her jeans and pulled them up over her shorts. Then she scrunched up her face and laughed out loud. She was a funny girl.

"Why are you laughing?" he said.

"You are so serious," she said.

"If there is a time you would like a favor, you can ask me," he said.

She began to cry. It was very sudden and it scared him. She was not loud like the gulls but her lips quivered and the tears filled her eyes and she hid her eyes under her elbow.

"Oh, no, no, no," he said. "Friends have no strings. You don't owe me."

She ran to her bike.

"You're doing okay," she called. "You're doing superior."

She disappeared through the trees, like buttermilk on bread as his mother would say.

35

OLIVE

Olive heard the sound of Lise's car. The engine warned it was coming like a storm as the car rumbled into the Ronans' driveway.

"Hurry up!" Olive blasted from the porch. "We have to go now."

Lise was never to be hurried up. She stretched her legs out to the concrete. She was fully made up with her eyeliner and red lips in a white dress like she had someplace to go, and it wasn't Olive's.

It was only the second week of summer vacation and both of them had been on a job for three days.

"Where are we going?" Lise sauntered up the walk.

"Gabe's. I can't take my bike. I've got stuff."

Olive was wearing a white sort of cocktail-party dress.

The skirt had curls of fabric so it floated around her hips when she ran up the stairs in her flip-flops.

"I'm almost packed. Hurry."

"Why are you dressed like that?" Lise did not hurry.

"Why are *you* dressed like that?"

"I have a date."

"I'm getting married."

"Are you sure?"

"I mean not with a ring. Figuratively. I was always going to spend weekends at Gabe's this summer."

"You need a ride? Don't you need Gabe?"

"He doesn't know."

"Olive. This is not you. What are you doing? Besides it's not the weekend. It's a plain Tuesday."

She followed Olive into her bedroom that had a green glow and the sun shone in, and where Olive had a roller bag half stuffed on her bed. It was bigger than an overnight bag. Shirts, jeans, chargers, paperbacks, hairbands and everything Chris ever gave her were in a jumble beside the suitcase.

"Help me get this in the car," Olive said.

"Stop, Olive. Talk to me. Does it have to do with the accident? Tell me what's going on. I'm in the dark here. What happened to the grandfather?"

"He didn't do it," Olive said, firmly pressing clothes in her suitcase. "Gabe was driving the truck and he kept the legal distance a vehicle has to be from a bicycle. Mr. Paudel was on the wrong side of the street and kept zigzagging. I've done that, trying get up our street." She wouldn't look at Lise.

Lise paused. "I meant the grandfather."

Olive glanced at her as if Lise had said something cruel. "I don't know."

Olive stuffed in everything she could.

"Why are you taking all this stuff for the weekend?" Lise said.

"There weren't any charges. Gabe didn't do it."

"I didn't say he did. I said I was in the dark."

Out the window and across the street, the neighbors had turned the low leaning fence into a clothesline with Bhim's small shirts drying. There were many colors.

Olive and Lise bumped the suitcase down the stairs.

Olive said, "I've been going to marry Gabe since I was seven. I had my first conversation with Samir ..." She paused. "Lise, it was just two weeks ago. Gabe didn't change in two weeks. He did some stupid things. Loyalty is when you stick with somebody."

"But he doesn't know you're coming?"

Olive shook her head. "How can I throw him away? He's all I want."

They moved like two bodies with a prisoner out to the porch and rolled the suitcase out to Lise's car. They stopped and looked across the street because something was going on. Cars pulled up. They watched as more people came.

"They have more relatives than I ever had even when I had a father."

They loaded the suitcase in the back seat. Lise emptied out the trunk, Olive removed the wheels from her bike, and they wrestled it into the trunk.

"Olive, stop. Just stop. You don't have to do this today."

Olive put the wheels in the back seat with the roller bag.

"What's true today," Lise said. "That's not going to disappear. It'll be true tomorrow. This feels like you're running from a fire."

They stood back and looked at the full car.

"You never liked Gabe."

"That's not true. Just that everybody's different since last summer."

"Let's go."

"You're the boss."

They got in, slammed the car doors.

They drove out of Creek Village. They had to drive through the west end where the split levels were going up. Where Kyle was probably on a ladder cursing the neighbors' dogs or whatever. They drove a curved street past Kyle's worksite to the highway.

Lise blasted Taylor Swift.

She glanced at Olive and rolled down the window. It got stuck halfway but still let the hot air blow in as they built up speed on the highway. Not far, but a lot of traffic. When she pedaled, there were loops of back roads.

"You tell your mom?" Lise said.

"She likes Gabe." Accusingly, her eyes straight ahead.

Suddenly they heard a loud *BOOM* that came from somewhere around the hood, and the boom blasted through the whole ancient car.

"Goddammit," Lise said.

Then they heard a whoosh and the entire right front of the car sank toward the road. It took no longer than a heartbeat.

After the boom everything unfolded in slow motion.

"Tire popped," Olive said. "Whatever you do, don't brake."

"You mean a blowout?" Air whooshed out of the tire.

"You're supposed to keep up the tire pressure. Especially in a relic car like this," Olive said.

"That's helpful," Lise said. The car tugged hard to the right.

Olive gripped the wheel to steady it. "Go straight. Keep it straight. Don't brake."

The car kept jerking to the right. Lise touched the brake.

"Take your foot off the brake. Don't let it spin out." Olive's voice was surprisingly calm.

A truck behind them blasted its horn.

They heard the *thud thud thud* of the front right tire hitting the road.

They slid onto the strip of a shoulder and toward a tangle of yellow-blooming weeds on the edge of a gulch.

And stopped.

Lise sat with her head in her hands, her chest heaving. Olive felt in control for the first time.

"Good job," she told Lise.

"Kyle's last revenge," Lise said through her fingers. "He probably knew the socialist was coming and emptied a box of nails on the road."

It was a whole lot closer to Chestnut Street than to Gabe's.

"Can we drive back on this tire?"

They couldn't. They found the spare, but they'd dumped out the bag of tools to fit Olive's bike in the car.

"I can change a tire, but I need a jack," Olive said. They

were both still wearing their white dresses. "We have to get it home."

"You want to call Gabe?"

"This is not how it was supposed to be. It was supposed to be easy and everything good would all fall into place."

"Oh, Olive."

Eventually, Lise remembered somebody with a tow truck, so that's what they decided to do. Get a tow back to Olive's and then change the flat. Her tow-friend came and mounted up the car, but he wouldn't let them ride in the back of the cab.

They were left sitting on rocks by the side of the road.

Lise said, "I'm late." She sent a text.

Olive said, "I'd have been there by now and everything would have been all right."

"Oh, Olive," Lise said.

They called Lise's mom, who came after a long time. She drove the girls to Olive's house.

The car was waiting for them. It was along the low, mostly level part of the driveway at Olive's house, looking embarrassed. Olive changed her clothes, found the tools they'd left by the walkway, put on the hand brake, jacked up the car. She threw all her attention into the lug nuts that were rusty and took all her muscles and shoulders and groans to loosen.

"You'll need to get a new tire," she told Lise when she was done.

"You want me to drive you back out?" Lise said.

Now it was late afternoon, and gray clouds kicked up and swarmed the sky in dark swirling splashes. Olive just looked up and it felt like the clouds lowered themselves on her chest.

She shook her head. She let the emotion of everything fill her. Chris's head heavy in her hands, Hajurba dancing at the farmers market, Gabe's hands on her thighs and her saying, *I don't know what to do.* Simone's child voice, *I'm a star. White people are gonna break free.* Samir's stupid swimming trunks. Gabe holding her, *Come home.*

Her body began to shake and she let huge sobs fill her chest and then between the sobs, awful gasping breaths. She ran around to the back to the fledging garden where Mom had been working since the rose came. She bent over by the rose and a bunch of other flowers and wept huge body-wrenching cries into the grass and the dirt.

Lise came and sat cross-legged beside her. Above them the swarming sky.

Olive hugged Lise. They both cried, until finally Olive stopped shaking.

Lise stood to leave.

"I'm putting your suitcase on the porch," Lise said.

"Inflate the tires," Olive said.

36

SAMIR

Samir and Bhim had seen Lise's car leave and the car towed back. After Lise drove it away, Samir sent Bhim on a job. Go to Olive's and invite her to come to eat. She would not say no to Bhim. From across the street, Samir could see a suitcase on the porch. His relatives including Heera were so busy at the restaurant with Baba and Uncle. The house was quiet.

When Bhim knocked on Olive's door, no one answered. He knocked again and called her name.

Eventually she leaned out the open kitchen window. Samir couldn't hear her. He heard loud Bhim.

"Can you come out?" he sang to her.

He showed her a dance move. In leaping steps he flew from the chestnut tree to Olive's glider swing with his arms reaching toward the sky.

He let his arms drop, grabbed the arms of the glider and crossed one leg over the other.

"Auntie wants you to come over," Bhim shouted. They carried on a conversation, but Samir couldn't hear any of it. And she hadn't come out the door.

Finally, when Samir looked again, he saw Bhim holding her hand. They were coming.

At their porch, Bhim kicked off his sneakers and waited for her to kick off her flip-flops. The cat had followed them across the street.

Samir opened the door.

"We are preparing to open the restaurant," he said. "Auntie would like you to taste one of the dishes."

Auntie greeted Olive. "Namaste, namaste," she said. She talked loudly over the drums and flutes from the dance video playing on the screen. Samir turned the sound down, but they could still hear the music in the background.

"I cook," Auntie Geeta said.

She guided Olive in. Samir saw their house as Olive might see it. The room was small. His family's shoes were in a row by the door. The yellow bicycle leaned on the wall. A Ganesha was on the side table beside a glowing candle. His aunt wore gold in her ears and beads around her neck and metal bracelets around her arms.

He wasn't sure Olive was so impressed with gold as Samir was.

In the kitchen, Auntie pulled a teapot from the burner. "We eat," she said.

Olive said, "Just a taste. Is Mr. Paudel coming home?"

"Yes, he is coming."

Right now, Auntie wanted to know if the dish was spicy or too spicy. Samir lifted the copper handle and poured tea into three metal mugs and passed them around. He sat on their large soft couch in the living room. Olive and Bhim sat beside him. Olive looked very weary.

On the TV, Prashant Tamang sang.

"Ama and Auntie like this singer," Samir explained to Olive. "All Nepali people like him. He is a Tamang from Darjeeling. He was an Indian Idol."

Auntie dropped her hands to her hips and swayed to his music.

Olive was quiet. She was not the same way she was at the cove.

"He is singing a lament in this movie, *Gorkha Paltan*," Samir said. "He is told to go for a soldier, and he is promising love to his bride, even if he cannot return."

Olive accepted a warm plate of food Auntie brought to her.

"What do you think?" she said to Olive.

Bhim brought roti and also a bowl of chutney.

"Cilantro, garlic, lemon," Auntie said.

Samir said, "Ama said that customers will often ask, so we should tell Americans the ingredients of the dishes."

Olive sank into the couch.

"I haven't eaten all day." She ate some tarkari. She smiled at Auntie but it was a very small smile. She was not hungry. "Could I take a little to my mom? She loves spicy food, and she could tell you the number for spiciness."

Bhim turned up Prashant Tamang on the TV singing his sad song.

"I would like one more lesson," Samir said, finally finding a moment to talk about what he most needed to ask. "For freestyle."

Olive seemed to think a very, very long time before she answered.

"I can come at three."

"Yes, three."

Bhim called out, "Now come with us to take Hajurba's dinner."

After they ate, they prepared to go to the hospital. On the porch, Olive's cat slept beside the chicken roost. The chicken was beside him in the chair. Olive wrapped her cat in her arms so she could take him home, along with food for her mom, who had come home from work.

Samir drove them all in Uncle's car to the hospital with Auntie as the required adult, and Olive and Bhim rode in the back seat.

At the hospital, Hajurba sat in the tall chair he had in his room. His feet didn't reach the floor. No tubes. A snake of stitches on his head. The head wound was the only injury the doctor had found.

Samir put the plate of warm tarkari and roti covered in foil on his table.

Olive showed Hajurba her phone.

"Lord of the Fishes," she said, even though Samir had already shown him the picture.

Hajurba took the phone and squinted at the image, then put on a pair of glasses to look some more. He sighed and sat back.

"You drew him," she said.

"Horse," he said. He gave her the phone, then said something in Nepali.

"Okay," Samir said. "Auntie and Bhim are waiting in the car because Bhim fell asleep on the ride. We will not stay long.

He turned to Olive. "Hajurba wants to draw you something. Drawing is how he talks to his teacher and he wants to talk to you."

"Why?" she asked him.

"He says you're lonely."

"I'm not lonely." She turned her eyes away like Samir had done when Hajurba said you need seven friends.

Hajurba's head was slightly lowered and his voice was hushed. Samir told her the words in English, but soon it was as if only Olive and Hajurba were talking. They kept their eyes on each other. She moved closer.

"He wants you to understand his grandfather's family was very, very poor. They were people who dug farmland out of the foothills of Nepal. Very hard farming."

Olive sat at the foot of Hajurba's bed so she could see the pictures. Hajurba drew a wide river in his school notebook Samir had brought him. And also three colored pencils.

"He said a rich man came to offer jobs to his father and others in his Nepali village. The jobs were in Sikkim. In Sikkim they paid for work with money. In Nepal you have to pay the government taxes to let you work your own land. But in Sikkim they needed laborers to clear the land for more cardamom fields. They paid Indian rupees. It was a chance like gold."

Hajurba's voice was almost a monotone and he hardly

paused, but he glanced up at Olive at key times as he spoke. Samir saw he liked telling her his story.

"That's how our family began to move for work from Nepal to Sikkim to Bhutan. We were famous for our hard work. And they would pay! They say, Come, Nepali farmers. They say that in Sikkim. They say that in Bhutan. Come, Nepali farmers. Come across the river. That's how we became Bhutanese."

Hajurba drew the outline of a horse — the same outline he drew before.

"My family built a farm in the hills of Bhutan. We had animals on the farm." He drew goats, sheep, oxen, a horse, pumpkins, himself and his wife in their square jackets he made red and yellow. A farmhouse with a turquoise door.

"Is this a true story?" Olive said.

"True?" Samir asked his grandfather.

Hajurba yawned. His eyelids began to fall. "All true. And the horse is good luck."

Samir helped his grandfather stretch out under the covers to sleep. He poured water into his glass with a straw. He lifted his own hands to his forehead and bowed.

Olive stood by the door.

"Why do you think horses are good luck?" she said.

Hajurba said, "Because horses know how to find the way home. I know this because my horse came home to my wife when I was detained."

Olive said, "Samir is learning to swim. You should see him."

Hajurba flashed his eyes on Samir with a glint of happiness.

"Not yet," Samir said. He was solemn. She shouldn't have said it. But he liked the glint. It scared him. He could fail. But from the day he couldn't put his head in the water, he had practiced the strokes with his arms in his mind's eye. "I am learning to stay on top of the water. And when I am not practicing in the water, I dream it."

A slow nod of his grandfather's face. Then he closed his eyes.

Samir drove Auntie, Bhim and Olive home, imagining doing the swim strokes as he drove. He could feel it in his midsection muscles. He imagined how they flexed when he swam and how they would help him withstand the force of the water. Or another's force. Every day he was feeling his body more powerful in the current.

37

OLIVE

The next afternoon Mom came home right behind Olive. Gabe had fixed the alternator on her car.

Olive could have asked her mother to take her out to Gabe's. Her suitcase was still on the porch.

But she didn't. Mom and Olive skirted the suitcase at the door.

"Yesterday I was going," Olive said.

"But today you're staying?"

"Mmmm."

"Don't surprise me. Talk to me." Mom's hand touched the strap. "If you can't talk to me, well, just sit with me."

Before long Mom was mud-caked in the garden. She was transplanting more seedlings into the dirt.

Olive watched her mom dig, still in the khaki work shirt

she wore with shorts. Her hair fell down her back in a braid. She stood up in the garden, the blue of the sky around her when Olive came out.

Olive sat on the bench that swayed. Mom sat on a bucket.

Gabe had texted her at work Monday. She didn't answer. Tuesday she was going to live with him, then her heart cracked because she couldn't go through with it. Now today.

"My stomach aches."

"Is Kyle part of it? Julia said Kyle was staying there while he was so sick." Mom looked at her straight on. "I don't know what's going on with you."

"It's only partly Kyle."

"But if it's Kyle, Gabe could come here."

Olive cringed. Across from Samir?

At suppertime, she decided she didn't need to put on the white dress and go out there. What she needed was talk.

She took a long, slow shower and put on jeans and the little wraparound gauzy top that tied with a string.

She wrote, "Can you come?"

When she saw him on her front porch, she swung open the door.

In one arm, he held a blown-up dolphin float.

"It's from the Day Night," he said. "You said you wanted the dolphin if we went to Jackman."

"I remember." She let him in.

He put his hand on her ribs over the little gauzy top. He pressed her to the door and kissed her slowly.

She ran her hands down his shirt to his jeans, and there

they were again, the only two people in the world who could understand each other. They made love on the couch, fast and hot, knowing this wasn't the best place in case Mom came down, but that made it too intense and too good to stop.

His cheek smelled like soap and she wanted them to lose themselves in each other for the rest of the night. She felt the roughness of his jaw.

Afterwards, he rested his hand on her chest.

"Could we talk?" he whispered.

She shook her head not yet, and they kissed. She liked his hand by her heart.

Her phone went off and jarred them. She turned the phone off. She slipped on her gauzy shirt and jeans. They went into the kitchen and Olive pulled on her holey sweater and pulled the hood up over her hair, and she loved the night breeze through the window.

They sat at the kitchen table. In the center of the table was a lemon pie Mom brought from the market but no one had eaten yet. The tangy scent was a bite in the air.

"Olive, talk to me," he said.

"I almost came out yesterday. I'm packed." She gestured to the door.

"I saw," he said. "We can put it in the car."

The car was their car.

"Can I explain some things," he said.

"I don't want explaining."

"You don't know. Look at me," he whispered. He was sun-glowed and brawn like the summer he and Chris had worked on Johnny Greer's boat and Gabe paid the taxes on his mother's land from the earnings.

He reached to her and Olive felt his hands on her face and his fingers comb through her hair and it felt like the sweetest tenderness she would ever wish for. She closed her eyes.

"I wished it could be just you and me. That's why I thought we needed to get out of here."

He took her in his lap and the tenderness hurt.

But then she said, "They're afraid to talk to the police."

"I told the cop everything," he said. "I gave him space." He said it softly. "That's the law, three feet from a bike."

"I know. You said." She didn't want to say the same things. "But how could it hurt you to come to the hospital and see him? It was you and him in the accident. You could say sorry."

She felt the breach in her body. His pulling away.

"Or come to the house and see how his family is. Ask what they need."

The cat cried at the door and Olive stood to pick him up.

"Have you ever thought when things are bad here," Gabe said, "you take it out on the wrong people?" She could see him trying to hold on. "You can't come over and take it out on my sister. She said you pushed her when you came for her birthday."

"I wouldn't push her." Olive remained standing. She remembered putting her hands on Simone's shoulders where she stood by her dirt bike, wanting to see her face when she said Samir would be deported. She remembered that Simone stepped back from her.

"Why are you defensive?" He shrugged. "She's a kid."

"This isn't about you and me. This is about a family who moved into the neighborhood."

"It's all about you and me." Gabe had stood, too. He shoved his hands in his pockets. "Look, there's nothing we don't know about each other. We don't have secrets."

"Who said we have secrets?" Olive said.

"Simone told me she saw you with that kid."

"I'm teaching him to swim."

"You weren't swimming," Gabe said.

No, they had been laughing. They weren't thinking about it being June and all the things that hurt Gabe and Olive so badly.

"I didn't come over here to fight," he said. "I want to help you."

"You are twisting things," she said.

The cat leapt to the table, and she shooed him away.

"It was a terrible accident." He used the word each time. That night in the truck, he had also said he was in a rage. "I'm sorry for the guy."

Olive stood in front of him with her lips pressed. She was cut in half by the moonlight.

"I mean, it's not a secret this is no place for them," Gabe said. "We don't owe them anything. We go over and fight for them in their countries and then they come and take our jobs."

"We don't have soldiers in Bhutan."

"Now I'm a liar."

"It's just a fact that we don't. Please, Gabe." She said this slowly, so slowly. Because if he left, her world would end.

He kept on. "I'm not a racist. I just know my family came

from nothing. Today everything's about color, but there's more than color. I don't want him hanging around your house. I don't want you swimming with him." He still didn't shout. He walked to the doorway, stopped there and turned back. "We could have the world."

She sat with the bright pie again. She pulled her feet up to sit in a ball.

"What about what you and Kyle did? What about the window and the bike? Maybe there are other things."

He shook his head of sandy curls, and he was that little boy she'd grown up with. He sat down and shuffled his chair over to her and took her hands.

"Look," he said, "I think we both want the same thing. I think we both want to find a way to get back like we were. Don't keep giving me these tests. Don't judge me."

"I'm not —"

"No, listen. You said no secrets. You can never say I'm not honest. I'll tell you what happened. It was like self-defense. My dad found the old man and his kid trespassing at his worksite. Probably looking for whatever they could lift."

"Gabe ..."

"So everything that's happened is a warning," Gabe said. "From the beginning when he threw the brick at the window. That's all he did. Saying what's mine is mine. Just back off. Don't come around."

His voice kept going.

"Don't you see? I'm trying to help you. A few times we messed around with ways to warn them."

She sat back.

"We have to protect our own. If we had something for us

here, your brother wouldn't have died. He had a job but no insurance. He had a job which meant he wasn't sick enough to get treatment that insurance would have covered. This country's got so many ways to screw you."

"You hate the neighbor that much to blame them?"

"Olive, don't," he said.

In the kitchen, the pie was like the moon. Street sounds came from the open window.

"Come on," Gabe said.

He took her hand and they went to the living room. They lay on the couch. She could feel his heartbeat. That was real. She was curled around him. Their bodies fit perfect.

"I'd do anything for my sister. I'd do anything to protect my people. I'd do anything for you."

She held her breath.

"People will come and go from this place," Gabe said. "They won't stay. Maybe they'll go back home. But this place is our roots."

She squeezed her eyes shut. *Please stop.*

"Holy shit, we're young," he said. "We haven't even started yet. We haven't even lived together yet."

It's what she wanted.

"I'll be here for your mom, too. That's how much you can trust me."

That night with everybody over for dinner, when he'd gotten so mad, he'd said, *I thought I could trust you.* What did that mean? To be the kind of person he wanted her to be?

"If you don't have your family," Gabe said now, "what do you have?"

Then he said, "You need to leave that kid alone."

"Why don't you trust me?"

He didn't answer.

"I'm not the same person as you, but you can trust me."

She got up and sat cross-legged beside him.

"Okay, you want to talk about Samir? Here's what's going on with Samir," she said. "I'm teaching Samir to swim. That's what I'm doing."

"No, that's not all you're doing."

"You think I'm not loyal," she said. "It's not about the politics you and Kyle talk about. It's so simple. Why can't you see? You know all the things you were to my brother?" Her voice had become low and fast.

"Don't talk about Chris," he commanded.

She stood. "All right."

"Why are you really doing it?" he said. "What's so simple that I can't see?"

How to tell him. She took all of Gabe Boudreau in with her eyes.

"It's not about immigrants or injustice or jobs. It's about this boy who lives across the street. We look out for each other. Like I don't want him and Bhim to drown. And I grew up like a fish so I can teach them to swim."

She could have said that Samir had nothing to do with Chris. Was that disloyal? To go someplace in her head away from her brother?

Could she say she liked to wonder, and not always know something for certain?

Could she say she was lonely?

No, how can you be lonely when you're in love? She held

up her hands. She couldn't explain to him.

All she said was, "Samir's my friend."

"So you want to stop seeing me?"

"I want you to trust me. Love me."

He said, "Where the fuck did you go?"

He was off the couch. At the door. Banging it open. The outside was dark and still and smelled sweet.

She remembered sharply that Samir asked if Gabe had hurt her. And for some reason she asked if Gabe had hurt him.

Then Gabe was gone. She slipped out the door. The car disappeared in the dark. She was left with a suitcase and a dolphin.

Her world was gone. She held the dolphin by the neck. On its head, he'd written, *Come home.*

38

SAMIR

This afternoon only Bhim went with Samir to the cove. Even Bhim could call 911 on Samir's phone. But he didn't need to because Samir swam the width of the beach.

He did not go fast. He felt the strength of his arms as he pulled through the water. His torso twisted as he lifted his arms and pulled into the green coldness. He didn't breathe in the water. Only pure air.

Then he swam out from the shore — not too far — and again. He stood and laughed and whipped back his hair that fell over his eyes while Bhim jumped up and down.

In the nights Samir dreamed the feel of his arms moving through water. When he danced, he counted his breaths like he breathed doing freestyle in the water.

Tomorrow he would swim away from the shore partway

and guess how many strokes to get to the island.

A clock was ticking.

He was going to swim. He was also preparing for Gabe.

Tonight he and Heera watched Gabe's red car pull away from Olive's house. He had watched the car for a few hours. He did not like to fight, but tonight in his mind he was a Gurkha, a soldier smashing the rear, slanted window of this car.

Heera brought him a persimmon fruit to remind him to swallow the yellow light. She was teasing. He was not. He practiced equanimity so he could swim with the next high tide and full moon at the cove. Olive said that was the best time.

Tonight they saw Olive come out on the porch. She stood in the shadows.

"Something is different with her," Heera said. "No music. She is quiet."

Samir saw only the outline of the girl. Was she watching the moon?

He saw the stillness, too. He waited.

Even his sister was silent. Inside, many people were sleeping on the floor in his house, waiting for Hajurba to come home.

Samir patrolled his house. He circled around to the back. Baba had installed a security camera on the corner of the house. He said they would have a security camera in the restaurant for the safety of the business. This is what they did in America.

Samir stood in the open space under the moon. He could barely see it in the clouds. The red dot of the infrared camera showed in the dark. A part of him yearned for the open fields in Nepal where he and his friends had been alone with the night sky.

On the edge of dark he heard the screen door slam across the street. He stepped forward among the trees near the street and saw the outline of Olive on her porch.

At the same time, he saw Heera jump down from their own porch steps and come to the fence of their yard. She opened the gate and looked across to Olive. He saw Heera's black hair that fell down her back. She wasn't wearing her glasses, but it seemed like Heera and Olive saw each other.

Then Heera clicked on a song from her phone and it played into the street. Samir knew the voice. It was that singer girls liked, Taylor Swift.

Olive came to the porch railing. Heera came to the grass by their gate. She was barefoot. The music had a rhythm that was hard not to feel in his body.

Heera began to sway to the music. She put her palms on her ribs and slid them down through the air. Then she reached to the sky and spun.

They didn't know each other. But his good sister had given Olive a song.

39

OLIVE

The rattling in the kitchen woke Olive from a dream. But it wasn't a dream. She'd fallen asleep on the couch.

She would not see Gabe today.

Last night the girl across the street had danced in the yard. She seemed to be saying hi across the leaning, broken fence. It was better than somebody talking.

But this morning sadness woke her up.

It was Thursday.

It was raining. It wasn't even camp day yet when she'd work in the art room. They'd sing camp songs around the forest houses the kids made from branches. They'd roast a dinner in tinfoil in a campfire.

It felt like some other girl's life.

When Olive pushed open the kitchen door, Mom was

there. Real estate brochures, cups of coffee, mini Drake's coffee cakes in cellophane wrappers covered the kitchen table.

She tried to make a cup of tea and not have to talk.

Mom kept her voice low. "I woke up at four with so many worries. Like I need a job that pays real money. We have value in the house. We have to get health insurance. There's things we need."

"You mean move?"

"I don't know. One of those 4 a.m. worries. You're going to be graduating in a year. I need to go back and finish my degree. Two years and I could do it. Would it matter." It wasn't a question.

Olive shoved her hands in her hoodie pockets and stared out the kitchen window into the awful gray light.

"We're lucky to have a house."

"I know."

"Is it because Gabe and I were talking about our own place?"

"No."

"Why, then?"

"I just woke up realizing I'm thirty-eight and I don't make enough money to pay the mortgage and help my kid go to college." Strings of hair fell over her mom's eyes. "No one's allowed to be poor and get by. You're just supposed to get another job."

"We can rent out the …" She couldn't say spare. Chris's room would never be spare. "… the bedroom. People at the shipyard rent rooms."

All these things were familiar about tight money. But it

came like a strike of lightning, the new ache in her chest that meant Gabe wasn't with her.

Could it have been a fight? This was like someone dying. Could he still be her boyfriend? Or was he not in her life anymore.

"How much money do we need?" she asked.

"I dreamed about the bathroom wall leaking and we had to wade through the water."

"Maybe Dad would give us some money?" Olive said.

"He does what he can."

"I'll help."

Two words on a sign came to Olive's mind. The sign was in the River's Tale window. *Help Wanted.*

The kettle whistled.

"Suitcase is still here," Mom said.

"Mmm," Olive said. She was dizzy with loss.

"You slept on the couch," Mom said.

"Mmm."

"What you earn this summer, it's for your college." Mom went into the bathroom and came back with a shoebox that she kept in the bottom drawer of the cupboard. It held every color of nail polish.

She leaned in to the tiered rows of iridescent, matte, metallic shades and picked violet.

"Mom, I can't." But Olive picked black. They hadn't done this since before Chris died.

"What do you do with that boy?" Mom asked.

"Which boy?" Olive shocked herself. There was only Gabe.

"The neighbor's boy," Mom said.

"Oh, Samir." The name was natural on her tongue. "I'm teaching him to swim. He wants to teach his sister. They don't swim in Nepal," she said. "It's landlocked."

"How's the old man?"

"He's coming home," Olive said. "I saw him at the hospital."

"I know. You think no one knows what you do?"

What did that mean?

"It's easier for us to talk about the new people than Gabe," Mom said.

Their eyes met.

"He's up against the wall with them," Mom said.

She turned away. Gabe was up against the wall but it was Olive who could not grasp how it got this way, or the ending.

She said, "Just so you know, Mom. We're keeping our house. We have a flower garden."

At 7:30, Olive called Ethel. There was a sister-thing with Ethel and Mom, and Ethel had probably already forgotten Olive shouting at the customers. To Ethel, Olive was entertainment.

"I could start Saturday," Olive said.

"Bus, dishwash, counter when I need you, 6 a.m. to 2 p.m. I need reliability — $13 an hour."

"I can work weekends for now. I work at the day camp, too."

"Weekends is when I need you. You and your brother were always reading in here," Ethel complained. "No reading."

"All right."

Olive calculated. She still didn't know what it would take to stop the rain coming in around the bathroom window. But with both jobs, she could at least buy the groceries.

On Saturday morning, Olive was late. Ethel was pissed.

It was 6:03 a.m. She threw Olive a purple River's Tale apron with the three swishing fishes. Matthew, the cook, had the grill spitting hot, sausages cooking. Nine people were already in the booths and at the counter. Nine! Why weren't they home in bed?

Ethel fired commands. "Stay here till the tables turn over. Coffee!" She showed Olive the pouches of premeasured coffee. The levers. The decanters of water. She had two kinds. Coffee and red-eye. The donuts came in on a truck. Olive unloaded them onto trays, the trays into bins. The smell was thick and heavy and it took all her strength and balance to slide the trays in.

The tables turned over. She loaded plates and silver into plastic bins. A girl named Barb was on the dishwasher. She wore jeans and a halter top as she worked over the steam of the power wash, hosing down the plates before she dropped them into the racks. She showed Olive how to hose them, set the timer on the big silver washer, where to stack the plates for Matthew so he had them by the right side of the grill. Olive got splattered with scraps and stickiness.

The dishwasher was where Olive would spend a lot of her time. That and on the floor busing.

"This'll scald you," Barb said about the water wand. "Make sure you keep the spout turned away."

Olive tied a clean new purple River's Tale apron over her top and went out to help Ethel clear the counter for the next batch of people.

By 6:30, Olive was exhausted. She loaded dirty dishes into bins. She wiped sticky juice and syrup off tables. Climbed under tables for dropped napkins and forks, a little brown-nosed bean-bag bear. She held the bear for a second on her arm.

A little girl in the next booth was watching Olive. Her parents weren't much older than Gabe. They talked in low voices like they had private, beautiful secrets. The mom said something and the dad laughed, pulled his cap back on his head. The mom had French toast. She held out a bite on her fork for the little girl, who now extended her hand to Olive. Olive gave her the bear.

She thought of Samir doing this all winter before school. Then in the summer he had worked through lunch.

At 10:55 they came in like any ordinary family. Gabe and Simone. They were arguing about where to sit. They must have ridden the bike in. He would have rocked the bike back to settle it on its stand. Lifted his helmet off. Dropped the gloves beside it.

She felt the drumming of the bike in her own bones.

When Simone saw Olive, she stared, still wearing her helmet, like a small belligerent Martian. She stood with her palms on her thighs and hip bones pushed forward. She wasn't the little girl who watched Olive with curiosity. They hadn't gone to Water Country or any of places Olive said they'd go in her origami birthday boat.

Gabe stopped in the middle of the café, surprised, like

what mysterious dark dream could they finally wake up from and become what they had been all along?

Then his face became steely.

Simone lifted her helmet and her hair spilled over her shoulders.

Ethel yelled out, "Two at the counter."

Gabe nodded to her. His eyes turned back to Olive. Olive had three tables to bus.

Simone asked for coffee. Olive slid behind the counter and poured her a cup. She knew Gabe didn't drink it. Gabe ran his hands over his hair, and then it stuck up like it did when he first took his helmet off.

"Why're you working here?" he asked.

Olive tried standing with her hands on her thighs like Simone. Then she dropped them to her side.

Gabe said again, hushed, "You don't have to work here."

As if they could have a secret conversation like the couple eating French toast with their kid.

That's when she nearly broke down, hearing him try to carry some of the weight. She must be showing she hadn't shut the door on him. She wanted to believe he'd been thinking about all the things they said. They could make something good happen for their families.

Isn't that what Samir said? *My family is my country. I am nothing without my family.*

"You have to pay," Olive said. She put her palms flat on the counter beside Gabe's elbows but she didn't raise her voice.

"For what?"

"For the Paudels' window."

"Forget about the fucking window."

People took a fast look at them, then turned away. He shook his head, and she saw his chin quiver.

Then he whispered, "You're bringing trouble to that family. They were better off without you."

"By asking you to pay for a window your family broke?"

Olive came slowly from behind the counter, wiggling her feet deeper into the flip-flops that Ethel said she couldn't wear anymore if she was going to work there.

At his side she whispered, "Come to the cemetery after you give them money to pay to fix the window. I'll see you there."

"Tell your Asian he should be on the alert." He spoke very low so people couldn't make it out. But she heard.

She felt like he'd knocked her on the floor. Your this group. Your that group. All of them. She felt a spark of fear in her stomach for Samir.

She walked, pressing her apron down her hips, to the first booth where she piled the dishes into the bin. The little girl had left the stuffed bear wedged between the seat and the wall. Olive put it up on the counter near the cash register in case the boy who was her father came looking.

She was clearing the table in the back corner and didn't see Gabe and his sister walk out the door without eating anything.

40

SAMIR

There were at least nine cars on Samir's driveway and grass and the street in front of his house. He tried to spot the movement of Olive's bike. He didn't know where she was or when she would come home.

That worried him. They had to finalize the plan to swim.

Many people had gathered to honor Hajurba's homecoming. He heard Heera call everyone outside because the priest had come. He was with Baba.

On the grass, Heera stood beside Ama and listened to the priest say blessings for Hajurba's health and strength. The priest chanted for a long time. Afterwards, he tied a yellow and red thread around Hajurba's wrist beside the rubber bracelet Samir gave his grandfather. The priest then tied yellow and red threads on everybody's wrists.

Samir came out to the gate to watch for Olive.

Music flowed from his front door and windows. Uncle had his arms in the air and he danced, and more relatives began to dance.

Finally, Olive appeared at the crest of the street. He called out. She squeezed on the brakes at his gate as if she needed to see him as urgently as he needed to see her. She stopped and took off her helmet.

He said, "I was waiting for you. We have to go. You said full moon and full moon is tomorrow. Tomorrow is the perfect day."

She was panting from coming up the hill. She leaned on the gate.

"I came to tell you." She took in all the people in his yard but spoke urgently. "We have to wait."

"It is the time," he said. "We said we would swim. Hajurba's home."

His grandfather was sitting cross-legged on the grass in a row of men. Aunties had brought them plates of food.

"We'll be swimming so far out," she said. "You're not ready."

He didn't understand. "I am ready."

"I took your job." She gripped her handlebars and did not look at him. She looked toward the music and loud voices coming from his yard. "I worked this weekend. Ethel will probably fire me."

Again, she was making excuses.

"I don't care about the job. I care about swimming across the cove. I'm doing this with you." A siren sounded far away. "Why are you afraid?"

She turned to face him quickly. He had accidently come to know her well, even while every circumstance and their lives divided them. He had seen her in many moods. But he had not seen her afraid.

She said, "Gabe and my brother were friends."

"But not now?"

"My brother overdosed. Gabe and I, my family, we tried so hard to help him. Gabe didn't get over it. He has these ideas about what killed my brother. People from outside." She held herself very tight and shivered — even her hands that wore no jewelry. "We can't swim, Samir. I'm afraid Gabe will hurt you. He'll do something. Not to me. To you."

Before Samir could answer, she was gone. Her bike was a blur as she crossed between the cars to her side of their street.

Samir waited as long as he could. Then he followed her across. He knocked at her door. He saw Olive's hand pull back a curtain from a window at the end of the porch. He walked to that window. Olive lay on her belly on a couch near where a breeze pressed the curtains into the window ledge.

"I wondered when your brother would come." Samir had sat down a short way from the window.

"He's not coming," she said.

He didn't know what to say. There was nothing more important than your sibling.

In a while he tried, "You said he liked the horse."

She lifted her head. Her fingers pressed on her lips like Bhim did sometimes.

"What do you want?" she said.

He saw the funny dark roots of her hair.

He wanted to be her friend. So he sat there.

"My grandfather wants to say hello to you."

"Tell him I'll see him tomorrow."

"He won't be here. He's going to Worcester to see a doctor."

"We can't swim," she said.

"I've been practicing," he said. "I can swim without you."

"I don't believe you," Olive said.

"I have a new job. Market Basket. They are good. Today I brought home five expired muffins." His face lit up. "I was tired every day of swallowing the yellow ball to have the peace to work with Ethel."

"Why are you happy?" she said.

"I'm happy because tomorrow we're going to swim across the Lord of the Fishes Cove." He was ready now. If he was afraid of Gabe, he wouldn't tell Olive. "I am stronger. I am ready. I need to do it for my grandfather."

"Gabe is not the same as he used to be. He hates you."

"We'll meet after work," he said. "At Market Basket, I work till five."

"Wait one week," she said.

"No, we cannot wait."

41

OLIVE

The tidal pool was best at high tide when the moon was full and the pool would brim with the incoming water.

It was Monday. Tonight the moon would be full. Olive pedaled to work at the day camp early. The sun was already warm. She was wearing a tube dress over her bathing suit top and shorts. She'd put more paint wax in her hair, so it was white with auburn fringe.

Suddenly Chris was right there running along beside her. He smiled. It made her heart race, but she smiled at him as if he'd come along just to see this pool made with rocks when the tide came in at the creek. The pool where you could settle your bones and float on the salt water.

She was positive she could touch him, feel the sweat he was working up as he ran, not missing a beat as she pedaled.

Nice look, he said, nodding to her outfit.

The material's stretchy so I can pedal. Hey, where do you want to be buried?

She slowed. *Don't go,* she thought. She wanted him to tell her.

He thought about this. He didn't go.

How 'bout back behind Gabe's house. You know, in the pine trees where the owls call.

They had never talked about this.

Do you want to know what Ms. Geeta said about love? she asked.

Sure.

She said it was like being a pumpkin hanging off a cliff.

Crapfire, he said.

Which side of the bike track do you want? she asked.

Straight back in the pines.

You care which tree?

Nah. I just liked the smell of the dirt.

Do you remember when you used to go fishing with Johnny Greer? You went out so early, it was about the time Mom went to bed sometimes.

Chris reached for the bumper of her bike and rested his hand there. She could feel the draw on her bike. He had a beard and looked just a little bemused by the situation he was in.

Yeah, he said. *We'd load up with bait and ice and steam out to Jeffreys Ledge to set the nets. Just us and nothing but the ocean and then the sun would blast up out of the sea.*

Olive pedaled down the rutted road to the camp. She circled around to the front where the camp building faced the creek. Chris was beside her.

I'll walk with you from here, she said.

This is the end of the road.

She stopped. *Don't do this again. Please, Chris. Not now. You've stayed with me so long. We're going down to the pool.*

She kept walking.

He hung out by the porch, bending over, his hands on his thighs, and panted from the run.

Those spoons, he called. *Put them away. Give them to your daughter when you have her someday.*

The idea hit her with brand-new grief at the length of her life without Chris.

But you won't be here, she said. *What about me? You're my brother.*

Get outta here, he said. *You're okay on your own. You always were. You were always the one who was gonna make it for Gabe and me.*

She turned a little. *Just come to the tidal pool.*

He shook his head.

He stayed by her bike. The stone steps to the pool were a dozen yards ahead.

It was when she was going forward that he disappeared.

42

SAMIR

When Olive came late that afternoon, Samir was already in the water. He was squatting and jumping up. Then he rolled onto his back and became still. He took in the late afternoon light. The tide was high. Even the long boulders they had run across were under the water.

Far away, kayakers passed under a bridge where the river moved hard to the ocean.

"Samir," Olive called.

He rolled off his back and stood. He was waist-deep.

She called, "Watch out. The rocks!" She swam out toward him. She was circling around the tall stones. "It's not that safe here. Where are you going?"

Samir was feeling light and had swum out farther and deeper. He was about thirty feet from the shore, swimming parallel to it. He had done this at high tide and low tide. He knew where the rocks were.

"Now you will ride the horse," he called to her.

She looked across. Lord of the Fishes had lifted his head.

"What do you mean, ride him?" Olive said.

"More than watch him. You can ride him," Samir called out. He swam toward her and then stood. He stood on one foot. He felt like a large New England bird. "He's going to hold you up in the sky. In the beautiful sky."

She leaned to him. She had wonder in her eyes.

"Samir, I never rode a horse. I draw them. I imagine them."

"Tonight you will ride one."

At that moment, she spun around at a sound in the distance. Like the rumble of a plane. But it was not a plane.

Then movement — a figure running between the trees. They both saw.

He was not surprised. It sent a jolt of fear through his body. And also a relief.

Finally it would happen.

Olive, though, swam like a racer between the rocks, yelling at him to circle away. She wanted Samir to run. Come ashore out of sight and run.

Samir needed to be on the land, but not to run.

He caught a glimpse of Olive's eyes when she looked back to him, wide and dark and scared.

He began to swim farther away from the shore so he could approach the land out of view. But he wasn't sure where he was going. His breath was shallow in his throat. This was a terrible mistake.

He wanted to show her he was a strong swimmer. And now he couldn't breathe.

He was swimming far out and over his head. He was seriously swimming long strokes but his arms were sometimes strong and sometimes failed him.

He would glide slowly, watching the riverbank for movement. He angled at first away then toward the shore.

"Swim in," Olive called. He saw her eyes scan the shore.

Samir focused his eyes on the distance ahead. Then he angled back toward a stand of trees where there was almost no beach, only rocks. He circled them, trying not to be a panicked dog with clawing strokes.

Gabe? Nowhere on the beach.

Samir was alone in the water.

Then he saw Gabe in the distance standing on the edge of a boulder that was all but submerged.

"Watch out." Gabe held his arms up as if Samir didn't already know about the dangers. As if he'd come to protect them.

Gabe knew the river, the rocks and the currents.

Samir's body began to shake in the cold water. In this river where someone could take your power, Samir spun in circles. He had not practiced his strokes while also preparing for someone to destroy the buoyancy of his body he had just discovered.

If he was going to protect himself from Gabe, it couldn't be in the cove.

He heard Olive scream at Gabe and he saw her race across the beach. She jumped on him and they both went down on the rocks.

"Leave the kid alone," she screamed. "It'd be like fighting a child in that water." They wrestled and she was screaming at him, "That's mean, Gabe. You were never mean. You're the one who changed."

They were rolling in the seaweed and stones. Now Samir knew *where* to swim. He torpedoed past the boulder to the point beyond where land jutted out, and cut in. He scrambled across rocks and then marsh and finally a thicket of trees.

He was out of the water.

The sun was still bright. It was quiet. Then he saw Olive lift herself to the rock in a leap, yelling with her hands in the air.

Samir shook, but he used those seconds to position himself. He dropped down among the brambles. He stopped. Filled his chest with breath.

"Gabriel!" Samir knew that was his birth name and he wanted to shout all of it. Samir said it loud, and his voice grew in volume.

"GabriEL!"

"Right here," Gabe said. He stood like a statue with his hands on his hips, though Samir did not think that Gabe could see him among the trees.

Olive shouted loudly to them both, "Samir, you don't need to do this. This is not your fight. It's ours. It's not even about you. You have to GO!"

Samir then ran through the trees and into the spot where it was both surf and land. Samir kept his focus on Gabe.

"I don't want to fight you," Gabe yelled.

At the same time, Gabe spun around and lunged, but

Samir sidestepped, ducked behind the wicked, jagged apple tree.

Gabe disappeared. When he called again, he was someplace different.

"Paudel!"

Gabe appeared from a thicket of brush and jumped on Samir's back, and Samir's whole body nearly gave way under the weight. But he slid forward out of Gabe's grasp and released himself into a patch of mud and sand.

Samir scrambled up, wiping blood from the side of his forehead and his nose.

Gabe disappeared in the low branches of trees. Samir was quick. Could he wait Gabe out?

Samir circled and appeared here and there through the trees.

"Paudel, you fucking rabbit! Get on your little bike and leave her alone."

She yelled, "If you hurt him, Gabe Boudreau, we're never going to have a chance to even fight with each other again."

Gabe leaped around her. Samir surprised him from the rear, nearly wrestled him down so they were both spitting sand. Then they chased and looped around each other down the beach, racing through marsh and water.

Finally Gabe leaped again and this time jammed his knee in Samir's back. Samir cried out. Gabe pinned him in the marsh now with his foot pressing Samir's shoulder blade.

Samir returned in his mind to the first time Gabe shoved him almost into the water. He had felt the hate in Gabe's hands. But now he knew so many ways Gabe showed him his hate. Samir felt the crash of his grandfather's body to the ground. Samir roared with the pain in his shoulder under Gabe's strength.

Then he dug his fists hard into the mud beneath him, enough to lift his chest and breathe deep into his ribs. He spun around when Gabe did not anticipate his fury.

In a split second, Samir drew his fist down, pivoted his torso, struck and slammed Gabe's jaw with one precise uppercut.

Gabe fell back on one of the rocks that circled them. Blood dripped from his jaw. He said something Samir could not understand, but he did not think it was any language, just hate.

He saw Olive approach. He saw her lean down. She had brought something to wrap the blood that fell from Gabe's face. Samir didn't know if he had splintered Gabe's bone, but he believed that if he stood and turned his back, Gabe would try to kill him.

Slowly he was aware of sounds around him. He heard a gull scream over their heads. Samir spit blood from his own mouth.

Then he stood, his hands on his hips, his jaw hard, his eyes harder, his chin lifted.

He looked at Gabe.

"You can call the police," he said. "They can arrest me. Or they cannot. What they do means nothing." He let himself drop down and sink into the rocks opposite Gabe.

Gabe was still holding his jaw, his blood soaking Olive's towel.

"I came to tell you something, asshole," Gabe said to Samir.

"Shut UP," Olive shouted.

"Do you know how much I care about you being arrested?" Gabe said.

Olive said, "You're talking so your jaw must not be broken."

Gabe's blood was on her hands. She turned to him. He lifted his head and let the blood roll down his Adam's apple.

Samir and Gabe moved around in their bones, their rib cages, their spines, their shoulder blades. They ran their tongues over their teeth.

"I came to tell you," Gabe said. "The current is strong." He looked at Olive. "Don't risk it."

Olive looked at the current. Beyond that, the horse.

Gabe scrambled up the short stretch of sand to the apple tree. He dug in his pocket for his keys.

"Olive, I don't have to fight anymore, and you don't have to do this. Come on," he said softly. "Let's go."

Samir pridefully turned his back and approached the water. He stepped forward and the waves washed over his feet, then his shins. He dropped down and felt the frigid water numb his wounded flesh. He was able to lift his shoulders and stretch his arms forward.

He saw Gabe keep walking, bearing more weight on his left leg. He was only a few yards from Olive, whose back was to Samir.

"I taught Samir to swim. Now he's swimming."

Samir heard the words she spoke.

"You're a good swimmer," Gabe said to her.

"You should go to the ER," Olive said.

Gabe studied her for a few seconds. Exhaustion fell into his eyes.

"Olive." Then, real slow, "I guess it's none of your business anymore what I do."

Olive stood in the wet sand like a tree.

When Samir looked back, he saw Gabe's solid runner's body disappear.

Olive waited. From a distance, he heard the dirt bike roar to life.

Olive spun and dived into the water.

43

OLIVE

The tide was high and the center of the current was a stripe of light and cold.

They swam. Olive could see Samir's arms pulling through the water. If he was terrified by the push of the water, it didn't stop him from driving himself through it. He was watching the opposite shore.

Olive shouted, "Aim for the path by the bridge."

"Yes," he shouted.

"But if we miss it, never mind. Don't try to swim across the current."

"Yes."

"Do a diagonal."

"I will," he shouted.

She swam long, slow strokes. She kept her mind on her

breath and her strokes. Then she couldn't see Samir at all.

"Are you there?"

No sound.

At that moment she felt the draw of the current. She kicked harder and harder against the current that wanted to pull her legs down. The surface was glass. The current wasn't strong, but enough to disrupt her stroke and take her breath if she was unsure.

"Swim with the current. Samir!"

The wind whipped up foam and for a while she couldn't see around her. She couldn't see Samir's arms or his head or which direction he had taken.

Something brushed her leg. A branch of a fallen tree? The rope of a lobster trap? Eelgrass?

She had gradually swum out of the current. She wasn't far from shore but the current took her farther down on the island, not near the bridge where she had told him they should go.

She swam close to the shore, on guard against slamming into the rocks or debris that could catch her legs and hold her down as the water rose.

It was suddenly quiet. She was alone searching the dark water.

"Samir!"

She found a birch tree leaning into the water and, with a foothold in the rock, pulled herself up through bugs and thorny dog roses to the bank.

She raced back down the island toward the bridge she'd overshot, scrambling and shivering. Ahead of her she saw the white boards of the corral.

"Samir, are you here? Samir!"

Ahead, she saw the low wooden bridge. And the boat launch and a path of pebbles to the bridge.

And Samir.

He stood beside the bridge, one knee bent with his foot on the worn wood of the deck, hands on his hips.

It was like the picture Mr. Paudel described of the prince of Bhutan standing at his school in America. Here, Samir was standing beside a sign that read *Private Property No Trespassing.*

His smile spread across his lips, crinkled his cheeks and turned his wide, laughing brown eyes luminous.

He pulled a cell phone from the pocket of his bright-colored trunks. He ripped open the plastic case that held it.

"I would be here sooner," he said, holding the case. "But I had to chase my phone in the water."

"What? You chased your phone in the current?"

"I swam," he said. He took her picture.

"You swam," she said.

"I've been learning since I watched you from the tree." He gestured across the cove. The tree was splotches of green on the jut of land that was the beach where Gabe was not.

"I'm sorry I hit your boyfriend."

My boyfriend, she thought.

Her eyes followed the waterways in all directions. She heard a snort.

"Look behind you," he said.

Olive turned. Lord of the Fishes. His nose was on the paddock fence.

She inched toward him.

"I've never seen him this close."

"You will ride him," Samir said again.

Impossible.

The horse stepped back. Olive climbed up on the fence and jumped over.

Lord of the Fishes loomed over her. He stepped back. His nose was long. He breathed in, trying to smell her. He made small awkward leaps across the field not far from her. His mane lifted in the air. She saw the little bristles of hair around his muzzle. She saw his eyelashes, she was that close.

"Holy crap, you have a beautiful head."

The white fence of the paddock circled the tumbledown school. Samir was in a maze of vines in an arbor of grape bushes with their tendrils spread over him.

They were both someplace they'd never been before. Olive ran toward Samir and when she stopped, the horse stopped. When Olive started again, the horse followed. When she stepped backwards, she watched his muscles move and his knees bend with his long steps.

One, two, three, four, each foot at a time. His legs were shaggy-haired. She studied him from his muzzle to his tail.

She could have spent hours watching the movement of this horse.

The horse still followed her.

"What do you think?" Samir called.

"No one so far has arrested us for being here."

"I think you should approach the horse."

They listened for any sound from up the road. No sounds. Just the horse who snorted. The water that lapped on the stone retainer wall.

"Do you know how to ride?" she asked.

He gave that shake of his head. "He does not seem too wild, though."

They started to laugh because the horse gazed at them with tranquil curiosity. Then he blinked at them.

"I think you lean on him first. You know, to get him used to the weight of a person. I read that," she said.

"Good," Samir said.

She gave him a crooked smile. Samir was enjoying this. They strode forward.

The horse's back rocked from side to side as he walked.

In *The Black Stallion*, the boy had first leaned into the horse's body before he dared to try to mount him.

Olive leaned diagonally on Lord. He didn't shift his weight or turn his head. He didn't seem to notice.

They walked to the stone wall at the edge of the shore. Lord followed. Olive leaned into his bony back again and smelled him. It was a good smell, maybe from the hay he rolled in. She wrapped her hands in his mane, which was coarse and warm.

"Do you want to hold him by the halter?" she asked Samir.

"Yes!" Samir said. But his words stumbled after that. He hadn't budged. "But I would prefer to swim than ride a horse."

"You're afraid?" Olive said. "Of a horse."

He came a little closer.

"That's better," she said.

"Is he going to rise up?" Samir said.

They both watched the horse, who let out a sigh and the

spots on his chest puckered. Together they led Lord in a curve and drew him close to the wall.

Olive jumped on the wall when they approached. The wall was a good height, and she carefully lifted her right leg over Lord's ribs and hoisted herself up on his back. She kept her eyes on his white bristles of hair.

"You look good up there," Samir said.

"Yes!" She clung with her chest to his back, her head in his mane. Her heart raced. She tried to find her balance. What if she pressed her legs into him too tight?

She tried to lift her eyes and see past his head. He moved. Then she realized that he had just picked up his right foot and that had shifted his whole body.

"I'm dreaming awake," she said as she lifted her gaze to the view from between his ears.

Slowly, she lifted her chest a few inches. Her arms loosened. Higher, higher. She clung with her fists to his mane.

Then she lifted her head inch by inch from his withers.

She whispered, "We are so enormous."

Then the horse took a step and she screamed and wrapped herself again around his neck. Samir walked along beside his head.

Lord took another step. Olive felt the shift in his muscles and tried to hold his body gently with her knees and thighs to sit lightly.

"I'll stay with you," Samir said.

He did.

She barely breathed. She allowed herself to lift her gaze again to the field, then to the trees, then to the sky.

Lord stepped forward into the field. Olive leaned over

his withers, her back straight, and held on with her arms. Was the horse responding when he felt the pressure of her knees? As he walked, her body surged side to side. She tried to balance again and feel the lightness upright, her spine a little longer. Olive rode with her arms woven through the strands of Lord's mane, and she was part of his smell.

Then she started sliding. She wiggled, pressed her knees into his bones to lift herself. But she slid and slid to the side, to his wide, round rib cage. She kept sliding, and the angle of her body took her straight to the ground.

She landed on her back.

"I think you're supposed to return on the horse," Samir said.

"Very funny," Olive said.

Lord stood beside her and snorted.

"Let's try this," Samir said. "I've seen it in movies."

He made a stirrup with his interlaced fingers. Olive stepped her left foot into his hands, grabbed hold of Lord's mane as Samir lifted her foot. She wrapped her right leg around, held tight to the mane and solidness of all the horse's muscles and inched herself to the top. And sank into him again. She squeezed her knees to his sides.

"I'm brave," she whispered into his spots.

They stepped forward again. Sometimes they moved forward. Sometimes she slid off.

Falling off and getting a lift up happened again and again. Olive was aware not just that Lord smelled like hay, but that Samir's hair smelled like salt water. And his arms and legs were strong.

Finally, she found the rhythm of Lord's movement. She

wasn't very big and she held on like a winding vine to his back. Lord was content to amble along with her limbs all around him, and she settled her bones into the rhythm of his bones. The warm wind blew on her bare skin.

Lord may have been thin and old and bumpy as he navigated the rocks and roses, but he seemed to want to keep her up there.

Samir watched from the arbor with his arms folded, that goofy smile on his face.

She called to Samir, "We're flying!"

44

SAMIR AND OLIVE

When Samir and Olive swam back across, the tide had begun to draw away from the shore. They could see the tops of the rocks that had been hidden beneath the water.

They hauled up on the other side and sprawled still as death on the long, flat, rock-exposed beach.

Their lives settled in around them.

Samir said, "I have been in a fight. I expect there will be bad consequences."

Olive said, "I was going to move to Gabe's."

She pulled her tube dress on over her swimsuit. Samir pulled his jeans over his garish trunks.

They lay there some more. There was more sand now where Samir and Gabe had beaten each other.

"Did you swim with a hurt shoulder?" Olive asked.

"I don't know. The water numbed it."

The air was warm. The sky had streaks of orange.

"I'm sorry that your heart is broken," he said. She had not said it was, but he knew.

"Thank you," she said.

Their stomachs growled. The warm breeze dried their salty hair.

"What will your father do to you?" Olive said.

"He's going to be very disappointed in me."

They were silent.

"We had a story in the refugee camp," Samir said, hugging his knees, and now and then a shiver passed through him. "It was about a temple. The temple has a locked door and inside that door is a sacred chamber with another locked door that leads to a chamber more sacred than the one before. And inside that chamber is another locked door to a chamber even more sacred and only certain people have the key to the doors."

"Where do the doors go?" Olive asked.

"I don't know. They were a secret. Until you got in," he said. "It was about who had the right to the key to enter the secret places."

She rolled that idea around in her mind.

"What made you think of that story?"

"I think I opened one."

"Okay."

"The door to having a friend. But when I got that door open, there was a door within."

"What was behind that one?"

"I didn't want what I found. But it helped. How to be

American when you have to. You don't show this side to your family. For the first time you have a secret from your family."

"You mean having to fight."

He looked at her, then ran his hands over his head to feel the blood and knot.

"You swam the river," she said.

"Yes," he said. "I'm still kind of delirious."

"Me too," she said. "Do I smell like a horse?"

"Very much," he said. "Is it always this hard to make a friend in America?"

"God, I hope not," she said. "And I have a Bhutanese friend."

"Nepali," he said.

"Whatever."

"I can't go home," Samir said, suddenly solemn.

"What do you mean?" she asked.

"Because of the fight. I can't tell my father."

"When he sees your face, he's going to know."

"Yes. That is why I can't go home."

"If you didn't go home, where would you go?"

He didn't know. They lay back on the rocks and looked at the mighty streaks.

"Maybe Gabe will report me as a troublemaker."

Olive said, "Gabe's family keeps a mile away from the cops. They say the cops are the government. They hate cops."

"I know what my grandfather would instruct if he knew I fought. He'd say, 'Here is what you do. You ride home. You eat. You must eat Nepali food to give you back the blood you lost to the river. Then you have the courage to face your father. You say, I am a scholar. Didn't you post my picture and boast when I am on the honor roll? For these things, your father will forgive your bloody face."

A text came in on Samir's phone.

"It's Auntie," he told Olive. "She and your mom are looking for us. Your mom couldn't reach you. Your mom wants to know when you're coming home."

"I don't have my phone. Would you tell them I'm coming?"

He did this.

Then he said, "Baba wants me at the restaurant. He will pick me up downtown."

"When?"

"Now."

Olive gave Samir her baseball cap to cover his eye. The knot above it was turning purple.

"Pull it down low," she said. "It's big as a gull egg."

After Samir left, Olive waited at the cove. She sat on the rock and took in the changing colors around her. It was too dim to see the horse. She hoped someone had come to bring him supper or take him back to his barn.

Again she thought about Chris saying that the land they lived on was just borrowed from the sea. She pictured the curves of the river as it flowed through the city, farther on the dog leg in the river where a fishing boat slid through. In her mind she saw where the cove met the river and the river met the ocean. She saw the vague shapes on the island that she knew were the old school buildings the nuns ran and also the spotted Lord of the Fishes. The finger of land her house was on. The fingers of land in the salt water that touched all the world.

Right now, she held her fingers to her mouth and produced the purest sound — a whistle that pierced across the cove like an arrow.

HISTORICAL NOTE

The novel *Go Home* is grounded in the backdrop of a Bhutanese Nepali family resettled as refugee immigrants in northeastern US.

The immigration of Nepalis and Indians to Bhutan helped populate the southern frontiers of Bhutan by 1958. They were called Lhotshampas — people of the south. They were naturalized, but considered second-class citizens by the ruling elites.

Culturally, the Bhutanese new Americans are closer to Nepalese and Indians due to their faith (primarily Hindu, as in present-day Nepal). Some aspects of their culture reflect generations of living in Bhutan and their proximity to northeastern India.

In 1989, the regime in Bhutan implemented the suppressive One Nation One People (One Culture) Policy requiring the Lhotshampas to accept the language (Dzongkha), faith (Buddhism) and traditions of the ruling elites.

In 1990, demonstrations against the Bhutanese regime caused many Nepali-speaking leaders and activists to leave the country for fear of incarceration. By 1993, more than 100,000 had fled or been expelled. The refugees spent seventeen to twenty-five years in one of the seven UNHCR-organized camps in eastern Nepal.

Between 2008 and 2018, the US, Canada, Australia, New Zealand, the UK, Norway, Denmark and the Netherlands resettled 115,000 individuals. About 6,600 remain in the camps, expecting to be repatriated to Bhutan. The children born in Nepal could technically be called Bhutanese as Nepal never considered them Nepali by birth.

Praja Shapkota, PhD

AUTHORS' NOTES

Lochan Sharma and his family are among the first Bhutanese Nepali people I met while working with New Hampshire Humanities literacy program to support new Americans. They worked with us to create a bilingual Nepali English picture book, *The Story of a Pumpkin*, by Hari Tiwari and Dal Rai. Lochan's parents, Ambika and Hari Sharma, and his sister, Lochana, are all part of the creation of *Go Home*. Lochan's great-uncle, Praja Shapkota, a scholar, also contributed as a consultant on history and language. Dr. Shapkota left Bhutan after being detained as a human rights activist. He lived in Beldangi II camp in Nepal for twenty-one years, volunteering for UNHCR and teaching across the border in India. He came to the

US in 2013 and now has a PhD from SUNY College of Environmental Science and Forestry and Syracuse University. He lives in Syracuse, NY.

Terry Farish

Samir and I are both Nepali immigrants whose parents are from Bhutan. My family is connected with Timai refugee camp. Samir lived in Pathri/Sanischare. They are both in southeastern Nepal. I've always liked telling people my history and where I come from but never really had a good way of sharing it. Writing this book with Terry was the best thing that could have happened.

Lochan Sharma

Terry Farish is the author of *The Good Braider* (YALSA and SLJ Best Book for Young Adults), *Either the Beginning or the End of the World* (Maine Literary Award) and *A Feast for Joseph* (with OD Bonny and illustrated by Ken Daley). She lives in Portsmouth, New Hampshire.

Lochan Sharma was born in Nepal. His family was registered in Timai refugee camp after they were exiled from Bhutan. He moved to the US in 2009 and now lives in Concord, New Hampshire. He is a student at Keene State College. This is his first book.

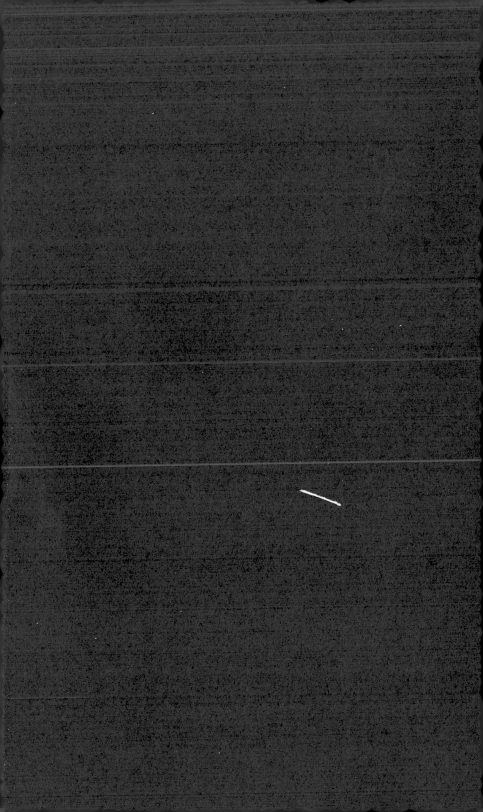